# everybody
# bugs out

## leslie margolis

**BLOOMSBURY**

NEW YORK BERLIN LONDON SYDNEY

First published in the United States of America in May 2011
by Bloomsbury Books for Young Readers
Paperback edition published in May 2012
www.bloomsburykids.com

For information about permission to reproduce selections from this book, write tó
Permissions, Bloomsbury BFYR, 175 Fifth Avenue, New York, New York 10010

The Library of Congress has cataloged the hardcover edition as follows:
Margolis, Leslie.
Everybody bugs out / by Leslie Margolis. — 1st U.S. ed.
p.        cm.
Summary: Sixth-grader Annabelle realizes that she has a crush on Oliver,
with whom she is doing a science fair project, just before the Valentine's Day dance—
and just before her friend Claire announces her crush on him.
ISBN 978-1-59990-526-6 (hardcover)
[1. Interpersonal relations—Fiction. 2. Friendship—Fiction. 3. Middle schools—Fiction.
4. Schools—Fiction. 5. Family life—California—Fiction. 6. California—Fiction.]  I. Title.
PZ7.M33568Eve 2011              [Fic]—dc22              2010035628

ISBN 978-1-59990-828-1 (paperback)

Book design by Nicole Gastonguay
Typeset by Westchester Book Composition
Printed in the U.S.A. by Quad/Graphics, Fairfield, Pennsylvania
2 4 6 8 10 9 7 5 3 1

All papers used by Bloomsbury Publishing, Inc., are natural, recyclable products
made from wood grown in well-managed forests. The manufacturing processes
conform to the environmental regulations of the country of origin.

**books by**
leslie margolis

## The Annabelle Unleashed series

*Boys Are Dogs*
*Girls Acting Catty*
*Everybody Bugs Out*

❦

## The Maggie Brooklyn Mysteries

*Girl's Best Friend*
*Vanishing Acts*

*For Lucy*

everybody **bugs out**

## chapter one
### duckwalk, anyone?

"Ready for school?" my mom asked me bright and early on Monday morning.

"Yes!" I couldn't help but shout. Enthusiasm is my middle name. Well, it is for today, now that I've officially survived my first semester of sixth grade and an entire winter vacation. That means I've got one semester down and only one more to go until summer.

But don't get me wrong—normally I'm not so giddy about having an entire school week ahead of me. It's just that I knew this term was guaranteed to be a gazillion times better than the last. Why? Well, for one thing, I'm no longer Annabelle Stevens, the shrimpy new sixth grader at Birchwood Middle School.

Okay, technically, my name has not changed and I'm still one of the shortest kids I know. And obviously I'm still in the sixth grade. But everyone knows that second semester is a whole different ball game. Meaning I'm no newbie. I'm older. I'm wiser. And I get to walk to school on my own.

Okay, not by myself, exactly. Mom says I'm allowed

to walk rather than hop a ride with her as long as I walk with a friend. And lucky for me, I've got two great friends in the neighborhood—Rachel and Yumi.

That's why I was up so early—showered and dressed, sitting at the kitchen table and ready for anything.

And speaking of being ready . . .

"What's up with breakfast?" I asked. "Because Rachel will be here any second."

"Coming right up," my mom called. One of her New Year's resolutions was to cook more often than never, which is her usual. So far, that meant a home-made breakfast for me every morning this year.

True, the new year was only three days old, but who's counting?

Besides me, I mean.

"Here you go." Mom dropped some fluffy scram-bled eggs onto my plate and then added two strips of sizzling bacon. "Waffles will be up any minute."

"Waffles, too?"

"Well, frozen waffles," she said.

"That's even better!"

My mom laughed. "I'm glad you're so enthusiastic."

"And I'm glad I finally get to walk to school."

I dug into my eggs, sensing my mom's look of concern from across the room. "Now, you're sure that you know how to get there," she said.

"Thataway!" I stifled an eye roll and pointed to my left. "It's only two turns and twelve blocks from here. We went over it in the car and on a map. And you already asked me to repeat the streets to you three times, and last time you assured me we were done."

"I know, I know," she said, flicking some stray egg off her sweater. "Just promise me one more time that you'll be careful crossing streets."

"Someone get me a mirror!" I said, gripping the edge of the table with both hands, my voice full of pretend panic. "Because I think I must've morphed into a first grader overnight."

My mom served herself some eggs, then slid into the chair across from me. "I'm sorry, Annabelle. I know you're always careful. It's not you I'm worried about, I promise. It's all those drivers. You can't assume they're going to see you. People are so distracted these days. Some even have the gall to text message while driving, which studies have shown can be more dangerous than driving drunk!"

Blahdy, blah, blah . . . I didn't say this out loud—I'm not *that* rude—but those are the exact words that ran through my mind as I wolfed down my eggs. Good thing I hurried, too. I was just swallowing the last of the bacon when the doorbell chimed.

As usual my scruffy black-and-white mutt, Pepper, was way ahead of me. Meaning he heard the bell first and had already raced to the entryway, barking like crazy. I swear, he must think that every time the doorbell rings it means a gigantic box of dog treats is being delivered. (And for the record—that's never happened.)

"Doorbell!" called my stepdad, Ted, as he came into the kitchen.

"Yeah, Pepper has already alerted us to that fact."

"Well, good morning to you, too!" Ted said, tugging at my blond ponytail, which was already in serious danger of coming loose.

"Hey, watch the hair!" I called as I hurried my dishes to the sink.

"Enjoy your first day back," said Ted.

"Thanks," I replied. "See you tonight. I've gotta run—I mean walk. Carefully!"

"Thanks for humoring me," Mom called as she handed over my lunch bag. "And have a wonderful day!"

"You, too." I rushed out of the room.

"Come on, let's go!" said Rachel as soon as I opened the front door. Before she said hello, even. Which is typical of Rachel. She always knows what she wants when she wants it, and she's not afraid to say so. Ever. Also, she's not exactly known for her patience—or subtlety—but that's not necessarily a bad thing.

"I'm all set, but what's your hurry?" I asked, standing in front of Pepper so he couldn't jump all over Rachel. She's allergic to dogs, and the last thing she needed was to break out in hives on day one of the new term.

Of course, even if it weren't for her unfortunate allergy I'd feel terrible if Pepper got his fur all over

Rachel's new outfit. She looked super-cute in her purple tunic top, black leggings, and silver ballet flats. Her wavy dark hair was pulled back in a low ponytail, showing off matching purple studs.

Rachel's lips shone with pink lip gloss, and her eyes shone with giddy anticipation.

"I already told you. We've gotta get there extra early on the first day back after winter break because there's so much to catch up on!"

"Oh, yeah. I forgot." I wasn't about to question Rachel's wisdom. Not when she's been living in West-lake forever and I only just moved here last August. "Cute outfit."

"Thanks," Rachel replied. "Yours, too. Great jeans."

"Christmas gift," I told her. "Actually, I exchanged the baggy, high-waist jeans my grandma originally got me for these."

She nodded with approval. "Good call. If only I could exchange my 'word-a-day' calendar for jeans."

"That would be awesome," I said.

"Or sublime. That's today's word."

Rachel lives directly across the street from me. Yumi's house is ten blocks away, so we walked five blocks to the corner of Easterly and Larchmont to wait for her.

Thirty seconds after we got there, Rachel frowned down at her new watch. It had a glow-in-the-dark sil-ver face and a purple sparkly band. "I hope Yumi isn't this late every day."

"School doesn't start for forty-five minutes," I

5

reminded her. "It should only take us fifteen minutes to walk there. And that's if we move super-slow."

"As long as Yumi shows up on time. Otherwise, we might have to speed walk, and that's no way to make a first impression."

"Speed walk?" I asked.

Rachel did a little demonstration, walking back and forth in quick but tiny strides while wiggling her butt and swinging her arms. "You know—speed walking. It's what some old people do for exercise. Instead of jogging or spinning or going to the gym like regular people."

I had to giggle. "I've never seen anyone speed walk like that."

"That's because you're not looking hard enough." Rachel wiped some fake sweat off her brow. "Picture me with a water bottle strapped to my waist. Oh—and skimpy spandex shorts. Some of them carry little weights in each hand. If you're ever at the lake in the early-morning hours, you can't miss 'em, because they often travel in packs."

"Um, you look like a duck."

Rachel stopped in her tracks. "Ducks travel in packs, too, which totally jells with my point. If Yumi doesn't hurry we'll have to duckwalk the whole way, which will make us the laughingstock of the entire school. We'll be known as those dorky duckwalkers for the rest of the year and maybe next year, too. Who knows? The name may even stick with us into high school."

"Yikes!" I glanced down at my own watch. Rachel's

anxiety felt more contagious than the chicken pox. Now I worried about being late, which would break my first New Year's resolution. And I'd only come up with four:

1. Don't be late for class.
2. Don't let anyone push me around.
3. Don't act catty.
4. Floss every night.

My track record wasn't so great, considering I'd already broken that fourth one yesterday.

Rachel huffed and stomped her foot. "Where is she? Jackson left when I did, so he's probably already there."

Jackson is Rachel's older brother. He's in the eighth grade, and kind of annoying if you don't know how to handle him properly, but luckily I do.

So far I've developed three strategies.

1. Avoid him.
2. Ignore him.

And if neither of those options is available:

3. Pretend like he's my dog, Pepper, and in need of serious training.

These techniques work on other boys, too. Not just Jackson.

"I doubt he's at school already."

"He could be because he took his skateboard," said Rachel.

"Which means he's probably hanging out at the 7-Eleven with his friends." That's what lots of the eighth-grade skaters do, and some seventh graders, too. Not something I needed to point out to Rachel, since she's the one who told me. "Ever notice how all those skater dudes travel in packs, just like those infamous duck-walkers you've been talking about?"

"Too true," Rachel said with a nod. "But there's less spandex and 'sweatin' to the oldies' music involved."

"That's what you think. But who knows what those guys do when we're not around."

Rachel cracked up. "I'm pretty sure they chow down on cherry Slurpees and Nerds every morning. If my mom knew, she'd flip!"

"You never told her?" I asked.

Rachel gave me a funny look, like I was wearing a vest made out of Brussels sprouts.

"Nobody likes a snitch, Annabelle!"

"But Jackson's usually such a jerk to you," I said. "Do I need to remind you of how, just last week, he secretly replaced your acne cream with toothpaste?"

"I know his intentions were bad, but in the end, he did me a huge favor!" Rachel stroked her chin, which had been pimple free for days. "I'd no idea that tooth-paste would be better for drying out my oily skin. Or that I'd smell so minty fresh!"

"Well, how about when he crashed your birthday

**8**

party and acted like a total menace? And have you already forgotten that he and his friends ambushed us with rotten eggs on Halloween?"

I didn't mean to harp on the negative. But this was Jackson we were talking about. The guy's got some serious issues. How else could I explain the fact that torturing Rachel and her friends seemed like one of his favorite pastimes?

"Look, I know my brother can be a jerk. But some of his teasing just comes with the territory. That's what big brothers do. And believe me, I'd love to see him get in trouble for buying junk food—and for a lot of other things, too—but like I said, I'm no snitch. And even if I were, I couldn't bring myself to break the brother-sister code."

"The what?" I asked.

"The code. I can be annoyed with my brother and trash-talk him like crazy and we can fight twenty-four seven, but if he's really in trouble, then I've gotta get his back. Just like he'd get my back if the chips were really down."

"Interesting word choice," I couldn't help but point out, "since he sprinkled all those potato chip crumbs around our tent when we tried to camp out in your backyard last month."

Rachel cringed. "Yes, I've never seen so many ants in one place, but I'm serious about the code. You need to know this stuff now that you have a brother of your own."

"Stepbrother," I clarified. The word still felt strange

coming from my lips, but I'd have to get used to it because my mom just got married to her boyfriend, Ted. And Ted has a son named Jason, who's twenty. He's studying abroad in Switzerland this year, so he doesn't live with us. "Jason's way too mature to bug me or pick fights."

"Maybe it's different with a stepbrother. Especially when they're brand new."

Rachel looked at her watch again, and then gazed down the street toward Yumi's, growing more impatient by the second.

I knew how she felt. Plus, standing around on the corner was getting boring.

"Think I should call her?" Rachel asked.

"Isn't your cell for emergencies only?"

"Yeah, but I'm pretty sure this counts." Rachel reached into her backpack.

"Wait, here she comes." I pointed down the street at the small figure running toward us.

"Sorry I'm late," Yumi said once she got close enough. She pushed her bangs away from her face. "I overslept. Guess I'm still on Hawaii time."

"How was the trip?" I asked, since I hadn't spoken to Yumi since she got back last night.

"Amazing!" said Yumi. "And check this out." She unzipped her backpack and showed us a Hawaiian lei made out of pink and white orchids. They were slightly crushed and a little brown at the edges, but still pretty.

"Awesome!" I said.

"I was going to wear it to school, but figured it's way too dressy."

"Good call," said Rachel.

"Although it does go with my dress." Yumi was right. Her sundress had a pink and white flower pattern on it—fresh flowers, not wilted, obviously. Her outfit seemed totally Hawaiian and very un-Yumi. I hardly ever saw her without jeans and a Dodgers cap. Usually she pulled her hair back into a ponytail, but today she wore two braids. I guess she wanted to look extra nice for the first day of the new term, too.

"I brought macadamia nuts for everyone," Yumi said as she carefully put away the lei. "But I'm saving them for lunch."

She zipped her backpack closed and we headed toward school.

"So tell us about the trip," I said.

"You got so tan!" Rachel said.

"I know! We went to the beach every day because my grandma's condo is, like, two minutes away."

"So cool!" I said.

"And last Thursday we took a boat out to this reef for snorkeling and we saw a shark!"

Rachel gasped. "That's so freaky!"

"It sounds scary but it was only a baby nurse shark. They're small, and pretty harmless unless pro-voked. At least that's what our guide told us. And no one got eaten, so she's probably right."

"I wish my grandma lived someplace good," said Rachel.

I had to agree. "Yeah, mine lives in North Hollywood. The most exciting thing to do near her place is bowl."

"I love bowling," said Yumi.

"Okay, I'll trade you—all the bowling you can stand for a week in Hawaii every year." I held out my hand, as if shaking on it would actually seal the deal. (And don't I wish it were true!)

Yumi crinkled her nose. "Never mind."

Just then we turned the corner and saw Birchwood Middle School up ahead. That tall pile of bricks had caused me so much angst and stress and general yuckiness last term.

Hard to believe, since this morning all I felt was excitement—and for a good reason.

Rachel was right—plenty of kids had gotten to school early. Most sported new-looking outfits and cute hairstyles. The halls buzzed with excitement. People hugged and laughed and shrieked as if they hadn't seen each other in months.

Rachel, Yumi, and I joined the crowd and, I must admit, I got swept up in the thrill of it all, too. And then I saw Taylor Stansfield.

Suddenly all the drama of last term came rushing back, like one of those super-scary tsunami waves that seem to hit from nowhere.

In one second I felt happy and carefree, and then in the next—not.

My stomach got all twisty and my throat went bone dry.

A silent alarm went off in my head and my molars started aching. (Weird but true!)

And as for my giddiness? It popped faster than a balloon in a field of thumbtacks.

## chapter two
### think there's no problem? think again...

If you don't know who Taylor Stansfield is, you obviously don't go to Birchwood Middle School. She's the most popular girl in the sixth grade, which means—as far as I can tell—that no one really likes her. Sure, people pretend to, but I think that's because everyone is secretly afraid of her. And that includes her best friends, Hannah, Jesse, and Nikki, a group that my friends and I used to call the Three Terrors.

Taylor radiates a bubbly and totally confident persona. She's pretty, too. And fearless—not afraid to stand up to teachers or talk to boys or do whatever she wants, whenever and wherever. On the surface, she seems like lots of fun. But once you get to know her you realize she's not exactly, um, nice.

I used to think Taylor was cool, and for a while it seemed like we were becoming friends. And then I learned the truth—the hard way. She's gossipy and backstabbing and kind of mean. Seeing her made me feel all nervous and prickly inside. Not scared, because

I knew Taylor wouldn't actually bite my head off. She'd just take a little nibble. . . .

Of course, my friends and I didn't act innocent, either. We were all kind of catty. That's how the tension grew and grew until it exploded, like some evil, out-of-control blob in a scary movie.

I couldn't repeat the drama this term, hence my most important New Year's resolution. No, not the one about flossing. It's this: don't act catty.

I repeated it to myself and tried to avoid looking at Taylor.

And I could tell that Yumi and Rachel noticed her, too, because we all got really quiet. Yumi stared straight ahead, and Rachel kicked a small rock on the ground. Not like they didn't notice—but like they were deliberately trying to not make a big deal out of seeing Taylor.

Two weeks is not a lot of time in real life, but when you're in middle school, it's a lifetime. That no one said anything about Taylor confirmed this.

As soon as we got to our lockers, Rachel let out a yell—alarming until I realized she was just excited about seeing Claire and Emma, our other best friends.

Claire is easy to spot because she's got bright red hair and she's one of the tallest girls in the sixth grade. She's probably one of the prettiest, and I don't mean that in a shallow way, just a factual one. She always stands out, too, because her clothes are so bright and colorful. Distinctive, or as Claire calls her look, "fashion forward." She's a super-talented designer—the girl can make an entire outfit out of duct tape. And that's including accessories and shoes.

Emma doesn't stand out so much, physically. She's regular height with big brown eyes and brown hair that she parts in the middle. She's more into books than clothes, and she's usually pretty quiet, too, unless you know her really well.

Yet the two of them are essential to our group. They balance each other out, I guess.

"Hey, you guys!" Emma said as she struggled to fit a bulky dictionary into her locker.

"Can't you just use the one at the library?" Rachel asked her.

"This one's more up-to-date," Emma replied.

"So great to see everyone!" Claire said, giving us all quick hugs.

"You chopped off all your hair!" said Rachel.

"Not all of it." Claire ran her fingers through her hair, now layered and shoulder length and bouncy instead of super-long. "I got bangs, too."

"So cute!" said Yumi.

"*Très chic*!" said Emma.

"Glad you approve!"

After everyone hugged like we hadn't seen each other in a year (see above for two weeks seeming like a lifetime), we compared Christmas presents. Which was Hanukkah for Claire and both Hanukkah *and* Christmas for Emma. Lucky her!

Everyone agreed that Yumi's gift was the best. Not

only did her parents take her to Hawaii for ten days, they also bought her a cute new cell phone—flat and silver with a pink and green striped case. "So pretty!" said Claire.

"Do you have unlimited minutes?" asked Rachel.

"I don't know." Yumi frowned at her phone. "Probably not because my parents said not to use it too much. Of course, they never said how much too much is. And I'm afraid to ask, because I might not like their answer. So I figured I'd just use it whenever and wait and see what happens when the first bill comes next month. That way, they can't really complain."

"Good thinking," said Emma.

"But be careful using it at school," Rachel warned. "If you get caught talking on the phone in class, your teacher is allowed to confiscate it."

"I know," said Yumi. "But does that count for texting, too?"

"I think so," said Claire.

"I've seen lots of kids use their phones at lunch," said Yumi.

"Lunch is fair game," Rachel said.

"What about in between classes?" Yumi wondered.

"Frowned upon but not forbidden," said Rachel. "That's the official word, anyway."

"Who are you texting, anyway?" asked Claire. "None of us have cell phones."

"I do," said Rachel. "Except I can only use it in emergencies."

"We know," said Yumi, Claire, and Emma at the same time.

"But why are you so worried?" I asked.

Everyone looked at Yumi, who seemed squirmier than usual.

"No reason," she said quickly. "I was just wondering, is all." She was quiet for a moment and then said, "I can't believe they could just take it, though. What if they scratched it? Or left it on and the battery ran out? Do you still get texts if they come when your phone is out of batteries?"

We all looked at each other blankly, no one knowing the answer.

As Yumi put her phone in its matching pink case, the first bell rang, so we headed to class.

When I got to English I said hi to Tobias, who sits behind me. I also smiled at our teacher, Mr. Beller.

Here's the deal with Mr. Beller: he seems like a tough-as-nails grouch, but if you stay quiet and don't cause any trouble, he's really not so bad. In fact, today he smiled back at me and asked, "How was your winter vacation, Annabelle?"

"Fun," I replied. "And yours?"

"Very nice, but too short," he said gruffly, and then sat down at his desk and began shuffling around some papers. "I barely had time to catch up on my grading, and now I've got to start all over again."

"Or you could just not give us any homework," I suggested with a sly grin and a one-shouldered shrug.

Mr. Beller glared at me, which is when I remembered that he's got no sense of humor.

"Kidding!" I added, holding up my hands.

I decided to stay quiet for the rest of the period. Sometimes it's just safer that way.

Class ended before I knew it. In fact, I made it through the entire morning without one snafu. Pretty amazing considering that back in September, I was brand new and intimidated—no, totally scared—about what I'd find in middle school.

I got lost. I got humiliated. And since I went to an all-girls school up until the fifth grade, I was totally inexperienced when it came to dealing with boys.

But today my whole morning flew by. I had social studies in an entirely different building—one I'd never been to all the way on the other side of campus, but I found it easily. In fact, I even helped one of my classmates, Justin Johnson, find his way there.

I didn't get lost.

I didn't get tripped.

Didn't get laughed at.

Nor did I use the broken drinking fountain—the one so clogged with gum that it only squirts a small, hard stream of water straight up. (Something I fell victim to three times last term.)

I knew which bathrooms were too gross to enter (all but the one near the music room).

And I knew which eighth graders to avoid. (Most of them.)

In short, I'd figured everything out. School was old hat, but not boring. I was comfortable. Happy. It was like I finally belonged.

At least that's what I thought before I got to lunch. That's when I approached our regular table and noticed all my friends huddled close and whispering to one another with urgency.

My stomach twinged with nervousness. Clearly my friends all knew something I didn't—never a good thing. "What's going on?" I asked, half fearing the answer.

"Valentine's Day," Rachel informed me.

"Um, isn't that in February?" I unpacked my lunch, still feeling uneasy but trying not to make a big deal out of it. Mom had made me a meatloaf sandwich— yum! And she'd packed pretzel sticks, carrots, celery, and two of Ted's homemade oatmeal chocolate-chip cookies. He'd just taught me how to make them and there are few things more delicious.

Not that I could appreciate them at the moment, what with the thick cloud of silence enveloping our table. All my friends stared at me with shocked expressions, like I'd said something crazy. Or had decided to wear that vest made out of Brussels sprouts again.

"What?" I asked.

"February is next month," said Emma. "And the fourteenth is only six weeks and four days away! Or forty-six days. And that's merely one thousand, one hundred and four hours from now. Which is—"

"Okay, I get it." I held up my hands, interrupting before she got carried away. Well, even more carried away. "We know you're a brainiac—you don't have to prove it all the time."

"What'd I do?" asked Emma, all innocent.

"Nothing." Rachel put her arm around Emma. "It totally makes sense that you'd be so excited about Valentine's Day. You're the only one of us who has a boyfriend."

"Shh!" said Emma. In two seconds flat, her cheeks matched her strawberry yogurt.

We all cracked up. "I didn't know it was a secret," Claire said.

"It's not," said Emma. "But that doesn't mean we have to talk about it all the time."

Emma didn't need to be so shy. Everyone knew that she and Phil Vandenheuver were going out. And everyone thought they made a great couple. Phil is in the physics club with Emma. He's the second-smartest kid in the entire sixth grade. (Emma is the smartest.) He's got sandy blond hair, a hamster named Einstein, and he's lactose intolerant, which means he'll never guzzle milk and then squirt it out of his nose—which was one of her ex-boyfriend's favorite hobbies.

It made complete and total sense that Emma would be excited about Valentine's Day. For her, the holiday probably meant gifts of chocolate or flowers. Jewelry or a cute stuffed teddy bear, or maybe jewelry *and* a teddy bear. Something cool.

But last time I checked, the rest of my friends were single. "So what's the big deal?" I asked, taking a bite off my celery stick.

I didn't mean to sound like the scrooge of Valentine's Day, but their excitement left me flummoxed. Bewildered. Completely confused. Absolutely— Okay, never mind. You get the picture.

"It's not merely Valentine's Day," Claire explained. "It's also the weekend of the first school dance. It's on Saturday, the fifteenth."

"Which is kind of anticlimactic," Emma said with a frown. "They should have it on Friday, the actual holiday."

"Saturday is better because it'll give us more time to get ready, and we won't be all tired and weary from school," Rachel said.

I pointed my celery stick at Rachel. "So you're going, too?"

"We're all going," Rachel said, sitting up straighter and smiling brightly. "We just need to find dates."

I finished chewing and gulped down my food. "Dates?" I asked. "You guys are kidding, right?"

Everyone just stared like I'd said something totally mixed nuts. And who knows? Maybe I had.

The thing is, I'd only just recently figured out how to deal with Birchwood's unruly boys. And now I'm supposed to find one to go to the dance with? Impossible!

## chapter three
### a date with mr. rainbow head

**Y**umi had softball tryouts every day after school that week, so Rachel and I walked home without her.

"It feels like we've been back forever!" Rachel ·complained on Wednesday.

"No kidding," I said. My back ached from carrying my heavy backpack and my mind ached just thinking about all the homework my teachers had already piled on. "So much for easing us back into the new semester! But it does seem rather extreme."

"Oh, I'd call it mean!" Rachel replied with a grin. "The pain in my back."

"It's gonna give me a heart attack!" I finished.

"At least it's a sunny day."

"Not that we have time to play."

"Probably won't until we're old and gray."

As of yesterday, we'd been trying to have rhyming conversations to make the walk home more fun. It was Rachel's idea—and a good one.

"So, confession time," said Rachel.

"That's easy to rhyme!"

"You know Erik?"

I thought for a moment. "Is he friends with Derrick?"

"No, game over. This is a serious question," Rachel said.

"Oh, sorry. The only Erik I know is one of the Corn Dog Boys."

We called all the guys who shared our lunch table Corn Dog Boys due to a disgusting incident that took place last semester—and one that I'd rather forget.

"That's the one," said Rachel. "He's the guy who showed up at school today with purple streaks in his hair."

"Right, and last semester he had blue bangs and then they turned green."

"Exactly!" said Rachel.

"Forget Corn Dog Boy. We should call him Rainbow Hair. I wonder what his natural color is. Think he even remembers?"

"His mom is a hairdresser and she likes experimenting on him with new dyes," Rachel explained.

"So there's a reason behind the weirdness."

"I think it's cute," said Rachel. "And guess what else? I like him."

"You didn't even give me a chance to guess!"

"Well, whatever. Not the point. So what do you think?"

I considered this for a moment, then turned to Rachel. "Maybe you should dye your hair pink. Then you guys would kind of match."

Rachel slapped my arm with the back of her hand. "Don't make fun of my new crush!"

"Sorry. Kidding! You're right—he's cute. And you should totally go for it."

"I'm glad you think so," Rachel said. "There's just one tiny problem. Minuscule, really, and it's something you could help me out with . . ."

"Sure, anything."

"I was hoping you'd say that! The thing is, I hear he's going out with Hannah and—"

"Forget it!" I interrupted. We were still two blocks from our street, but I stopped in my tracks. "I'm not helping you break them up! Hannah's my friend."

"She's more Taylor's friend than yours," said Rachel. "I know you guys talk at school but you never hang out on weekends."

Rachel had a point. Hannah and I were total school friends. And I wanted to keep it that way. "We finally have a truce with Taylor's crowd. So let's not mess that up."

"Relax," said Rachel. "I don't want you to try and break them up. Believe me, I learned my lesson last term."

"Good." I continued walking but remained skeptical. "So, um, how can I help?"

"Well, like I said—I heard they're a couple but I'm not positive it's true. So I thought maybe you could just ask her. You know—if they're going out. And if they're going to the dance together."

"That's *all* you want to know?"

Rachel nodded. "That's it."

It sounded simple enough, but I had to make sure. "And if they *are* a couple, you'll back off? No trying to steal him away? No bad-mouthing Hannah? No asking me or anyone else to get involved?"

Rachel gazed at me, surprised and hurt—like I'd really done damage to her feelings. "What kind of person do you think I am?"

"The kind of person who hates Taylor and all of her friends."

Rachel laughed. "Okay, that's probably true. But I won't try and break them up. This is all about Erik. I'm really into him and all I want to know is if he and Hannah are actually together, and if they are, I'll give up."

"Can I get that in writing?"

"Isn't my promise enough?" Rachel blinked at me like she couldn't figure out if I was serious or not—and to be honest, I wasn't sure, either.

But I'd take a chance. "I'll ask her tomorrow before French. Okay?"

"Awesome with cheese! Thanks!" Rachel held out her fist for a bump.

"No prob," I said as our knuckles hit.

When we finally turned onto our street, I waved. "See you tomorrow."

"Cool deal. And don't worry. I'll call Yumi first thing in the morning to make sure she's not late, again."

"She's been on time all week," I pointed out.

"That's because I've been calling her every day."

26

I laughed.

"What's so funny?" she asked. "Better safe than late."

"Said the sidewalk to the skate."

Rachel shook her head. "That doesn't make any sense."

"It doesn't have to," I said, looking both ways before crossing the street. "It's just gotta rhyme."

"Sure that's not a crime?" Rachel called from the other side.

Rather than answer her, I pretended to be a mime.

But I'm not sure if she got it, and if I explained, it would've ruined the joke, so I just let it go.

Once inside, I leashed up Pepper and took him to the park. After we played fetch for a while, I went home and started my homework, but I couldn't focus because I was too busy trying to figure out what to say to Hannah. So I decided just to call and get the "weird Rachel favor" out of the way, so I wouldn't have it hanging over my head all night.

Of course, I couldn't call Hannah only to ask about her supposed boyfriend. That seemed weird. So instead, I asked her if we had any French homework.

"We need to translate three pages of *The Little Prince* and also write about what we did over winter vacation," Hannah told me.

"Oh, cool," I said, pretending like I didn't already know. "That'll be easy for me because I hardly did anything."

27

"Really?" asked Hannah. "Nothing?"

"Well, my mom got married, and we celebrated Christmas, and I played with my dog, but we didn't go anywhere."

"Well, I went to San Francisco but didn't really do anything—just visited my grandparents and played a lot of Scrabble."

"Scrabble can be fun," I said.

"Not for ten days straight. The problem was, it was too cold to go anywhere good."

"Did it snow?" I asked.

"Nope. It just rained, as usual. I've never seen real snow before."

"Neither have I. Well, not more than a tiny dusting once, when we visited my uncle in Seattle, but I'm not sure that counts."

As we talked, I kept hoping the conversation would naturally drift toward boys or Valentine's Day or hair dye or even corn dogs—something I could actually segue into a question about Erik—but it never did, so I finally asked her, flat out. "Hey, are you really going out with Erik?"

"Yup," said Hannah. "Ever since New Year's Day. A bunch of my friends met a bunch of his friends at the mall, and we saw that new Ashton Kutcher movie and then he asked me afterward. By the fountain—the one people always sneak shampoo into?"

"That's awesome!" I said. "Not the shampoo part— that's just funny."

"I heard that last summer the fountain bubbled over and flooded the Gap."

"Huh." I squinted my eyes shut for a second because I felt weird about asking what I had to ask next. "Um, think you'll be going to the big dance with him?"

"Absolutely!" Hannah said. "In fact, I was just flipping through magazines, looking for outfit ideas."

"Cool! Are you going super-fancy or just kinda?" I asked. My friends had been debating this issue all week.

Hannah groaned. "I can't decide. At first I thought I'd be more comfortable in a regular dress. But then Taylor bought a strapless and now she's trying to convince all of us to wear strapless dresses so she's not the only one, but I don't want to stress about whether or not my dress will stay up all night, since it's not like I've got the goods to hold it up myself."

I laughed. "Yeah, I know what you mean."

"Thanks a lot!" Hannah said, seemingly offended.

"No, I didn't mean it like that, I swear! I was saying I feel that way myself—because I don't have the, uh, goods, either. And even if I did, I still don't think I'd get one because strapless dresses have always looked weird to me. Incomplete, like there's something missing."

"Like, Omigosh! I forgot half my dress!"

"Exactly. They should at least be cheaper since there's so much less material, but they almost never are."

We both laughed. Then she asked, "So what are you going to wear?"

"I don't even know if I'm going," I said, petting Pepper, who was lying next to me.

"You have to," said Hannah. "Everybody does."

"So did Erik ask you in person or by e-mail?"

"Neither," she replied.

"Did he text you?"

"Nope. I don't have a cell."

"So what are you saying? Did he get way old-fashioned and put a note in your locker?"

Emma sometimes gets notes in her locker from her boyfriend, Phil. Usually he writes short messages like, *Good luck with your Latin quiz*, or *Saw you walk by my class during second period*. Things that any friend could have written, but somehow, coming from a boyfriend made them seem better.

"Oh, he hasn't asked me yet," said Hannah.

"Then how do you know you guys are going?"

"Because we're a couple," said Hannah, like it was obvious. "He's not going to ask some other girl."

She had a good point. "Do all your friends have dates?"

"Not yet, but they're working on it," said Hannah.

"Your friends sound just like my friends," I said.

"It's not just us," said Hannah. "It's the entire sixth grade."

"No pressure," I added.

"Right." Hannah laughed. "But I'd better go. See you tomorrow."

"Bye."

After I hung up I thought about calling Rachel to give her the news, but I decided to wait until our walk to school the next day. But then I wasn't sure if it was okay to bring up Erik in front of Yumi. This was a sensitive issue, but my friends and I never kept secrets from each other before. Plus, Yumi was busy looking down at her new phone, texting someone and not paying attention to us at all.

So I figured it would be okay. But just in case it wasn't, I stayed vague. "I called Hannah last night. Turns out the rumors are true."

"So she and Erik *are* a couple?" asked Rachel.

I nodded.

"Do you know when he asked her?"

"Oh, he hasn't gotten around to that yet," I said. "But Hannah says she knows he will."

Rachel nodded, taking the news surprisingly well.

"You don't even seem upset," I was happy to say. I'd been bracing myself for the worst.

Rachel shrugged. "The dance is six weeks away. Even if Erik had already asked Hannah, well, a lot can happen between now and then."

I shrugged, not thinking about her words very carefully. But I should have. Because then I might have been prepared for the craziness to come.

Or maybe there wasn't any way to be prepared.

## chapter four
### no chicks, no turtles,
### and definitely no volcanoes!

A week later when I got to science class my teacher, Ms. Roberts, asked everyone to get right to their seats because she had some very big news. "Birchwood Middle School's annual Sixth-Grade Science Fair is in four and a half weeks," she announced, clapping her hands together and beaming as if this were the most exciting thing to happen to us since that pipe burst in the cafeteria and we all got a surprise half day.

I glanced around the silent room, clearly not the only one who failed to comprehend the importance of her announcement. I'd never heard of the Sixth-Grade Science Fair, and from the looks on my classmates' faces, they hadn't, either.

"If you're going to participate, you'll want to get started immediately," Ms. Roberts went on. "Choose a topic and, if you'd like, pick a partner or two. Just be sure to choose wisely because all members of the winning team will be awarded scholarships to Space Camp next summer."

As soon as Ms. Roberts mentioned Space Camp, practically everyone's hands shot up, and half the class shouted out their questions, before our teacher had a chance to call on anyone.

*What's Space Camp?*
*Are we gonna be graded on this?*
*Is the fair for the whole sixth grade or just our class?*
*Can I go to Space Camp if I'm afraid of heights?*
*May I please have the bathroom pass?*

Ms. Roberts smiled and held up a stack of pages. "Please settle down and hold on to your questions for just a few moments while I explain. This is a school-wide event, so yes, everyone in the sixth grade will be competing. The seventh and eighth grades have their own science fair, but you won't need to worry about that until next year. And all of the other information is right here in the handout. Please read through it before asking any more questions. Oh, and here's the bathroom pass, Caitlyn."

Wow, Space Camp! Could the news be more excellent? Actually, I wasn't sure, since I still didn't know what Space Camp was all about. Just that it sounded super-cool. Like, maybe if I won, I'd get to wear a silver space suit with one of those bubble heads and launch rockets and float around in a zero gravity chamber, drink Tang, and eat freeze-dried ice cream. Does Ben and Jerry's ice cream come freeze-dried? How cool would it be to eat chocolate-chip cookie dough in space? Too cool to calculate! And speaking of calculations, I wondered what my chances were, given that I'd be competing with the entire sixth grade.

I'd have to beat out hundreds of kids, which would be hard to do alone. I'm a good enough student—I can get As and Bs if I work really hard—but I'm no natural brain. So yes, I'd definitely need help. A teammate. I wondered if we had to choose partners from our class. Because if not—if we were allowed to work with anyone—I'd ask Emma. She's in honors science and she's the smartest kid I know. Not that she'd automatically want to work with me. Sure we were great friends, but she had her whole physics club crew to choose from, plus her boyfriend, Phil—another big Birchwood brain. They'd probably pair up and do something amazing and they wouldn't need my help at all.

The two of them would go to Space Camp together. Maybe they'd grow up to be real astronauts. They could be the first couple to be launched into space, have picnics on Mars, hold hands as they shot through the stratosphere . . .

Why would she pass up the chance to make history in order to work with me?

It wouldn't hurt to ask her, though.

As soon as the handout came to me, I scanned it until I got to the section on rules.

1. Original work is a must.
2. You may work alone or with up to two partners. That means individual entries or teams of two and three are acceptable. No teams of four!
3. Parents and siblings can assist when it comes to carpooling and shopping for supplies, but all work must be done by students and only students.
4. No student or team can spend more than $50 on materials. Hold on to your receipts. If there's any doubt, the judges will ask for proof.
5. Extra points will be given for innovation and creativity.
6. Do not miss the deadline. Everything must be completed and brought to the main auditorium on Thursday, February 13, by 6:00 p.m.
7. Judging will take place on Friday, February 14.

Friday, February 14, was Valentine's Day! Now there was even more to stress about. Or more to look forward to, depending on how you looked at things. (And as for me, I still hadn't decided.)

I read the rules again. Everything seemed clear enough. And better yet, there wasn't any ban on finding partners outside of class. Genius partners!

I wished I had a cell phone like Yumi and Rachel. If I did, I'd text Emma immediately, before she teamed up with someone else. Unfortunately, my mom and Ted don't find cell phones "necessary" at my age. And when I pointed out that lots of things were unnecessary (making me do the dishes and take out the garbage, for instance), they were not amused.

So I'd have to wait for class to get out. In the meantime, I made a mental checklist of everything I'd add to the team. No, Emma didn't need my brainpower, but I worked hard and I had plenty of other things to contribute. Out of all my friends, I'm the best at cracking corny jokes. Plus, thanks to Ted, I've almost perfected my oatmeal chocolate-chip cookie recipe. And everyone knows you can't work on big projects without a good cookie. Not successfully, anyway.

"Pretty cool, huh?"

I heard someone ask this, but I didn't think the question was directed at me until I felt a tap on my shoulder.

It was Oliver, my favorite lab partner. "I was just thinking about how excellent it would be if we won and got to go."

I nodded with real enthusiasm. "It'd be awesome with a side of cheese."

"Everything is awesome with a side of cheese. That's the whole point of cheese. To add to the awesomeness."

I grinned. "I never thought about it that way."

He smiled back. "Well, I have."

"Obviously."

"So should we go for it?" he asked.

"Wait, you mean you and me?"

"Sure, if you want to." Oliver shrugged and looked down at his scuffed blue high-tops. "Either way, it's no big deal."

"Okay, yeah." I said it fast, before I could really think about it. He caught me off guard, and yes was all I could think to say. It was cool of Oliver to ask, and if it weren't for the Emma possibility, he'd be the ideal partner. Oliver is plenty smart and hardworking. Sweet, too. He's quiet in a nice, kind of shy way, and he smells good, like unscented soap.

Okay, yes, his handwriting is a bit messy, but I like how he always uses both sides of the paper in his loose-leaf notebook. When he saw me notice this a few weeks ago, he was quick to point out that he did it to save paper for environmental reasons, not because he's cheap. Basically, he doesn't want to kill any more trees than he has to, which you've gotta respect. Or at least I do.

Anyway, my point is, there's a lot to like about Oliver.

Oh, and he's cute, too. Brown hair that used to be buzzed but now is a bit longer, but not puffy. He's got green eyes and dark skin and a nice but faint Jamaican accent that you really have to listen for.

"Perfect!" he replied with another smile. And that's

when I noticed how nice his smile was. It was the lack of dimples that put him over the edge. Oliver's smile was so bright he didn't need them.

So now it was settled. We were partners. I wondered if Emma would want to team up with us both, and I was just about to ask Oliver how he felt about working with her when Tobias, our other lab partner, leaned over and said, "I've got tons of cool ideas."

"Huh?" Both Oliver and I asked at the same time.

"We're partners, right?" he asked, narrowing his eyes at Oliver. "That's what you just decided."

In my head I screamed: NO WAY! THIS ISN'T HAPPENING! Because Tobias is basically everything that Oliver is not. His handwriting is very neat—small and boxlike—but that doesn't make up for his rude attitude. He's also annoying and loud and sometimes even a little smelly.

Today, for example, he reeked of stale sweat. Last week it was ketchup.

But I couldn't complain out loud. I didn't want to be mean and Tobias wasn't always that bad. We usually got along okay, but working with him on the science fair project seemed all wrong—totally unnecessary and annoying, too. Especially when I'd had my heart set on working—and winning—with Emma.

And from the uncomfortable silence that enveloped our table, like some stinky cloud of fumes from an experiment gone wrong, I sensed that Oliver wasn't happy, either. But he didn't speak up right away.

Not until Tobias looked from me to Oliver and asked, "What?"

"Nothing." Oliver coughed. "You're right. We should absolutely team up. You know, since we already sit by each other. It'll be easier that way."

Tobias nodded and Oliver nodded back. So I nodded, too, all the while trying to figure out how this happened.

Even though Oliver acted like he'd always meant to include Tobias, I didn't think he had.

I wondered if there was still time to get out of this.

It seemed unlikely, and before I could decide for sure, Ms. Roberts called the class to attention and started talking about cell structure.

At least she ended her lecture ten minutes before the bell rang so we could begin planning our projects.

By that time I'd calmed down a bit. I'd also noticed that most of the kids in my class were either working solo or with their lab partners, and that did make sense. Working with Oliver and Tobias maybe wouldn't be so bad. We were used to one another. And Emma probably had other plans, anyway. This was a good thing. At least that's what I convinced myself of before Tobias opened his mouth.

"We should hatch chicks," he said.

"Chicks?" I repeated skeptically. "That's not really an experiment. It's more like a project my kindergarten class did years ago."

Oliver laughed and Tobias just glared like I'd said

something mean, but I was only being honest. Okay, maybe my reply came out sounding a little too harsh. It's not Tobias's fault I didn't want to work with him. "I do like the idea of working with animals, though."

"Fine, forget the chicks," Tobias said. "How about turtle races? We can buy five of them and then feed each one a different diet and see how they do."

"Aren't turtles expensive?" I asked, pointing to the list of rules. "There's a fifty-dollar limit."

"Maybe we rent them," said Tobias.

"They're animals," said Oliver. "Not roller skates."

"Okay, what if we buy just one."

"A one-turtle race?" asked Oliver.

Tobias tossed his pencil into the air and tried but failed to catch it. "No, we can do something else with it. Dissect it, maybe."

"Gross!" I cried.

"I'm ethically opposed to dissecting animals," said Oliver. "And even if I wasn't, can that even be done? Wouldn't the shell get in the way?"

"Oh, I'm sure it can be done." Tobias bent down to retrieve his pencil. "Anything can be dissected," he replied, popping back up with a mischievous grin on his face.

Oliver and I looked at each other, wide-eyed and horrified.

"Kidding." Tobias threw his hands up in surrender. "Will you two relax?"

"Sorry." I shook my head. "But just the thought of dissecting something—egad!"

"No one really says 'egad' anymore," said Tobias. "If they ever did."

"Annabelle does." Oliver smiled at me. "And I think it's cool."

"Fine, take her side. I knew we shouldn't have teamed up with her!"

This was way insulting considering that Oliver had asked me first, but before I could say so, Oliver spoke up. "Dude, of course we should be partners with Annabelle. She's really smart and I'm sure she has tons of good ideas."

"Yeah, like what?" asked Tobias.

He and Oliver both turned to me, totally putting me on the spot. But that wasn't anything I couldn't handle. I'd already done some quick thinking. "Maybe we should do something space related. You know—to keep in theme with the Space Camp prize."

"That's what I was thinking, too!" Oliver's voice rose slightly with excitement.

"Everyone's going to do that," Tobias grumbled.

"Um, okay. Let me think for a sec. Oh—I have an amazing puppy named Pepper. Maybe we can try and teach him some new tricks."

"I'm allergic to dogs," said Tobias. "Cats, too. Anything with fur."

"Bummer," said Oliver.

"Well, what if we analyze different brands of dog food. Find out what's really in them. How healthy they are." I'd just read an article on the very subject. Turns out lots of popular dog food brands are not so great for dogs. And I kept meaning to look up Pepper's brand, anyway. Then I'd be killing two birds with one stone. Not that I wanted to kill any birds. Not even rhetorically for the purposes of science.

"That could be kind of interesting," said Oliver.

"Or kind of boring," said Tobias. "And I told you I'm allergic."

"To dog food?" I asked. "You wouldn't actually have to work with any live dogs."

Tobias shook his head stubbornly. "Forget it. Not interested."

"Fine." I took a deep breath and thought harder. "How do earthquakes happen?"

"Yawn!" said Tobias.

"What if we track the gestational process of a butterfly?"

"And you thought hatching chicks sounded immature?" Tobias said.

Okay, maybe he had a point there. But I didn't like how Tobias rejected all my ideas without even giving them more than a second of consideration, like he disagreed just because he wanted to be difficult. That was my suspicion, anyway. Meanwhile, Oliver stayed quiet throughout the whole process but kept looking at me and rolling his eyes, like he was running out of patience, too. I'm glad he was on my side but I wished he'd speak up.

"What if we track pollution in different parts of the neighborhood?" I asked.

Tobias made his "that sounds stupid" face.

I finally had to ask him outright, "Do you really hate the idea, or are you just saying no to all my suggestions because we rejected yours?"

"Let's make a volcano!" said Tobias, which didn't exactly answer my question.

"Huh?" I asked.

"We'll build a miniature one and also do a research paper on the history of volcanoes. You know—ones that have erupted and smothered people. There's one in Italy, I think. And Hawaii, too."

"My friend Yumi just got back from Hawaii. Maybe she has some pictures we can use."

Oliver shook his head. "No, forget it. We did a volcano experiment in the fifth grade. It's too easy. Just a matter of combining vinegar and baking soda."

"And red dye, so the explosion runoff looks like real lava," said Tobias.

"Right, I remember that from last year, too," said Oliver, clearly getting annoyed.

"Well, this will be better than that one. Bigger. Maybe we can use some miniature dinosaurs . . ."

"I thought you wanted to base the project on a real explosion," I said. "The one in Italy killed people, not dinosaurs. It's not like people and dinosaurs can exist at the same time."

"Or so people say," said Tobias.

"You are kidding, right?" I bit my bottom lip and tried to think of a good way to tell him his idea was the dumbest I'd heard all year. Maybe the worst I'd ever heard in my life. In a nicer way, I mean . . . "Dinosaurs just seem a little, immature . . . And the whole volcano thing, well, it's like Oliver said. You guys already did that last year. In elementary school. Elementary also meaning simple and basic. Childish, even." (Rachel wasn't the only one benefiting from her word-a-day calendar.)

"Whatever, Spaz!" said Tobias.

"That's not her name," Oliver said. At least I think he said it. The bell rang right when he opened his mouth, and then the room got so noisy, it was hard to hear.

"See you," Tobias called as he stood up and left.

Oliver waited for me to put my notebook away so we could head out of class together.

"Don't worry," he said. "We'll come up with something great. How about we all go to my house after school tomorrow?"

"Okay," I said.

"Great. I'll tell Tobias—make sure he's free."

"Great," I repeated, with exactly zero enthusiasm.

I didn't say what I was really thinking: so much for my grand plans of winning the science fair. With Tobias on our team, we may not even get the chance to enter.

## chapter five
### ladybug landing

The good news is, even if Emma and I wanted to work together, we wouldn't have been able to. She's busy with the physics club, volunteering at the library, and piano lessons on Mondays, Wednesdays, and Fridays. Meanwhile, my mom works late on Tuesdays and Thursdays, which means I have to come straight home to walk Pepper. We couldn't even meet up over the weekend, since I'd just signed up for karate, which happens every Saturday, and Emma has to spend Sundays with her family.

"It's too bad our schedules don't match up," said Emma once we finally got a chance to talk after school that day. "But you're lucky you have partners. I don't even know who I'm working with—if anyone."

"What about Phil?" I asked. "I thought you two might pair up."

Emma looked away, a slight frown on her lips. "I thought so, too. But he got weird when I asked."

This surprised me, since Phil seemed like a super-sweet boyfriend. On their two-week anniversary, he gave Emma a banana chocolate-chip muffin, and while that sounds icky to me, it's Emma's favorite kind. "Weird how?" I asked.

Emma took a deep breath and answered fast. "Well, we're both big science nerds and, as I pointed out, we could easily meet up after the physics club, but he said he wanted to do his own thing because he's got a better chance of winning that way. Oh—and he also told me that I shouldn't be offended because he's only being honest."

"At least he has good reasons."

Emma didn't seem very convinced. "Ever notice how whenever someone says 'no offense,' it's like they're compensating because what they're saying is, in fact, extremely offensive?"

"I never really thought about it," I replied. "I wonder what he's doing."

"Something involving his hamster, Einstein," said Emma. "But he wouldn't tell me what, exactly."

She seemed annoyed by this, and I didn't blame her. What kind of boyfriend kept secrets like that? "He's probably just worried that you'll come up with something better, which is exactly what you should do."

Emma shrugged. "I don't have any good ideas—except for cloning a fish, but that'll cost more than fifty dollars, I think."

"Probably," I said. "Why don't you work with someone else?"

"Yumi and Claire are in science together, and

they're already working with Hazel Feldman. But I guess I could check with Rachel."

"You totally should. And I'll be so jealous when you guys get Space Camp scholarships and I'm stuck at home all summer."

"Your group has just as good a chance of winning as the rest of us."

It was nice of Emma to be so encouraging, but I knew things wouldn't be that easy.

At least my group wasn't alone. Turned out lots of kids were having trouble coming up with a good project idea. It was all anyone could talk about in class the next day. Luckily, Ms. Roberts was able to help us out. Well, kind of. Being a teacher, she suggested a visit to the library.

"There are whole books devoted to science fair projects," she explained. "You can look online if you'd like, although I must warn you. There are also websites that sell entire science projects, and this is not just frowned upon, it can get you suspended. We have a zero-tolerance policy when it comes to plagiarism at Birchwood, so don't even think about using someone else's work."

"What if we accidentally plagiarize something?" asked Monique Parker in her strong French accent. Some people think it's fake because she was born in Missouri and only lived in France for a year when she was two, but I don't know. Her mother is from there.

"There's a big difference between using outside

reference materials and actually stealing intellectual property," Ms. Roberts said. "Basically, do not copy something word for word. And if you do use someone's idea, make sure to provide the appropriate reference. I've written out the specifics, because this is important. So please open your notebooks and write down the definition."

She turned on the overhead projector, where she'd defined *plagiarism:* To steal or pass off someone else's ideas or work as your own, or to use someone else's work without crediting your source.

Ms. Roberts coughed. "In other words, no cutting and pasting. Everything must be written in your own words. And if you come up with a project that you found in a book or online, mention that in the reference section of your final report. Is this clear?"

Oliver raised his hand. "What if you come up with something that you think is original but someone has actually done it before? Because haven't people been doing science projects for millions of years?"

"You've raised a good point, Oliver," said Ms. Roberts. "However, I think that millions of years is a bit of an exaggeration. The first science fair can be traced back to the 1920s and they became very popular in the 1950s. But yes—that's still a considerable number of projects. And there's nothing wrong with repeating an experiment that's been done before. I'm sure that will be the case with most groups. Some of you may enter similar or even the same projects, which is fine. What

I'm saying is, original work is a must. You must do the experiment yourself or with your partners and write everything in your own words. Okay?"

Everyone nodded except for Davis Peabody, who was too busy drawing pictures of monsters wearing tighty whities. (It's his latest thing—weird, I know. And speaking of plagiarism, kind of a Captain Underpants rip-off.)

"Now, if anyone has any further concerns, we can discuss them after class," Ms. Roberts said before going on to talk about cell structure.

As soon as the bell rang, my lab group made plans to meet up after last period so we could go to Oliver's house.

And before I knew it, the school day had ended and we were on our way. Oliver lives in Canyon Ranch, which is the rich part of town on the other side of school. It felt weird walking to his place, not because of all the gigantic houses we kept passing but because for the first time ever, I was walking to a boy's house—and going there with not one but two whole boys.

Of course, technically, Oliver and I were the only ones walking. Tobias had his dirt bike and he rode it slowly in front of us, circling back every block or two to complain about how slowly we were moving.

The thing that made the trip funny was how normal it felt. It wasn't that much different from walking home with Rachel.

There were no rhyming games, and we didn't talk about the school dance or about who was going out with whom, and we didn't compliment each other's outfits, but Oliver and I did talk about school stuff. Which classes he liked—English, math, and Spanish—and which ones he couldn't stand—social studies and stained glass.

"I thought those art classes were supposed to be fun," I said.

"Me, too," said Oliver. "That's why I signed up. But Jeremiah Lindy sliced open his middle finger on our second day of cutting glass and he needed six stitches."

"Yee-ouch!" I said.

"Yeah, I almost passed out when I saw the blood. Oh, and then Claire Macintyre burned herself with the soldering iron and had to go to the nurse. It wasn't that serious, but ever since then, just going into class kind of freaks me out."

"I can see why."

"What's your elective?" he asked.

"Chorus," I said.

"I should've signed up for that. Probably much less chance of getting injured."

"You'd think, but Jeff Diamond fell off a table and sprained his ankle last week."

"Why was he on the table?" asked Oliver.

"Why do boys do anything?" I asked before I remembered whom I was talking to. "Um, no offense."

Turns out Emma was right about her "no offense" theory. I just hoped Oliver didn't know about it.

Lucky for me he just laughed and said, "No worries. But I think we're onto something. Maybe we should do a statistical analysis of the dangers of electives at Birchwood Middle School."

"It's not the worst idea you've had," I said.

"Gee, thanks," he said, all sarcastic. "Oh—I forgot to tell you. I picked up a couple of books on science fair projects at the school library."

I grinned. "I tried to do the same at lunch but everything was already checked out."

"Guess I beat you to it. Good thing you're on my team."

"Oh, it's *your* team?" I asked, jokingly.

"Yup," said Oliver.

"Find anything good?"

"I haven't actually looked yet," Oliver said, stopping in front of a large house. Tobias sat under one of the palm trees out front, with his bike at his side.

"Took you long enough," he said, standing up and brushing the dirt off his jeans.

Oliver walked up the path to the front door and we both followed him. Once inside he called, "I'm home!"

Then a tall, skinny woman with dark skin and long braids walked into the entryway. She and Oliver had the same bright smile and similar accents, too.

"Hey, Mum," said Oliver.

"Hi, dear." She bent down to give him a kiss on the cheek and he didn't even seem that embarrassed about it.

"You have impeccable timing. I just got back from the grocery store."

"Cool." Oliver shrugged off his backpack and dropped it by the door.

"Hello, Tobias," said Oliver's mom.

"Hi." Tobias waved.

"And you must be Annabelle," she said, smiling down at me. "I'm Clarice. And I know you three have lots of work to do, so go ahead and get started and I'll fix you a snack."

Tobias and I followed Oliver to the den, which had all sorts of cool stuff—a gigantic flat-screen TV with a video game console, and train tracks for an electric railroad circling the entire room. I kind of wanted to see it in action but didn't want to ask. I was hoping Tobias would, but instead he picked up a mini Nerf basketball off the floor and tossed it at the hoop that hung on the other side of the room.

"Nice try," said Oliver as the shot bounced off the rim.

Oliver picked up the ball and swished it through the net, one handed. Then he raised his arms above his head and yelled "Victory!" Like he'd just been named the world-champion of Nerf basketball.

"Dude, that was a total lucky shot," said Tobias.

"Says you," said Oliver.

Tobias smirked and threw Oliver the ball. "Let's try for the best out of five," he said.

"Fine." Oliver caught the ball and immediately tossed it to me. "You go first, Annabelle."

Neither boy said anything when I shot and missed. Something I appreciated. But it still felt embarrassing. Problem was, I overshot because I wasn't used to the weight—or lack thereof—of the ball. But there was no point in making excuses. I tossed the ball to Tobias, who made the shot, and then he gave it to Oliver, who missed.

Luckily I made the next one and two more. Tobias and I tied and Oliver beat us both. Not surprising, since the hoop was his so he got to practice whenever he wanted. After the game, Tobias pulled down a strange, flat-looking paddle from the wall and began swinging it around.

"Careful, dude," said Oliver.

"What is that?" I asked.

"A cricket bat," said Tobias.

"A what?"

"It's a sport that's really popular back in Jamaica. More popular than baseball, even," Oliver explained.

"I think I've heard of it," I said, which was kinda true. "Do you play?"

"Only when I visit my relatives in Jamaica or in London, because no one plays here in Westlake."

"Are we going to figure out this science fair thing?"

asked Tobias, setting down the bat. "Because I've only got an hour."

Oliver tossed him a book and then gave one to me. "You guys take a look at these and I'll search online," he said, opening up a laptop I hadn't even noticed in one corner of the room.

I flipped through the book, which listed all types of science fair projects. There was stuff on astronomy, stuff on earthquakes, stuff on the digestive system of cows . . . All kind of interesting but nothing that really jumped out at me to say, "This is the topic that's going to propel you to Space Camp!" Not even the project on propellers.

"How about we do a project on recycling?" Oliver said a moment later.

I looked up. "What do you mean?"

"Like, what happens when we don't do it? You know—the whole global warming thing. Maybe we could create a melting glacier?"

"That's a good idea," I said.

"Monique is doing something on recycling," said Tobias. "Jonathan's group, too."

"Both of them?" I asked.

"Yep, and that's just in our class. All that environmental stuff is way too trendy. There's going to be a million projects just like it."

"Good point," I said, because it was. Maybe I'd judged Tobias too quickly. He wasn't completely clueless.

We continued to flip through the science fair project books in search of something original.

Tobias suggested an ant farm and Oliver nixed the idea before I had a chance to. "My brother had one of those once and it broke and all the ants escaped. It was a mess!"

A few minutes later, Oliver's mom poked her head into the room. "I hate to interrupt, but I couldn't help noticing how nice it is outside."

"Mum, we're trying to work," said Oliver.

"You can work outside," Clarice said. "And you may as well, since I already put some snacks out by the pool."

Once she was gone, Oliver stood up and stretched and said, "I'm sorry. She's always on my case about getting fresh air."

"It's no biggie," I said. "And it is pretty nice out."

We followed Oliver out to his backyard, which was huge, with a gazebo on one side and a big swimming pool on the other. The water looked sparkly and inviting even though it wasn't quite warm enough to swim. I took a step closer so I could get a better look at the rock formation waterfall but then stepped back, having momentarily forgotten that whenever I get too close to the edge of a pool I imagine myself falling—or being pushed—in. Don't know why, but I wasn't taking any chances.

Oliver sat down at a nearby table and we joined him. His mom had left us iced tea, lemonade, and a plate stacked high with three kinds of cookies: choco-late chip, ginger, and oatmeal raisin.

Good choices I thought, except for the oatmeal raisin. Fruit and cookies just don't belong together. I never understood Fig Newtons, either.

Oliver picked up an empty glass and asked, "Which would you like?"

Before I answered, Tobias blurted out, "Lemon-ade." Oliver poured it for him.

"What about you, Annabelle?"

"Um, can I have both?"

"Two drinks?" asked Tobias.

"No, I mean half lemonade and half iced tea."

"That sounds good," said Oliver. After he made my drink he made himself an identical one.

Meanwhile, I grabbed a ginger cookie and bit into it. "Wow, that's amazing!" I said.

"My mum's specialty," said Oliver.

"You mean she made this?" I asked, because few things impressed me more than skillful baking.

"Look out, dude!" Tobias yelled.

"What?" asked Oliver.

Tobias pointed to Oliver's arm, where a bug had landed. He raised his hand, about to smash it, when I cried out, "Wait, stop!"

Oliver jumped out of the way and shielded the bug with his free arm. "Back off, that's a ladybug."

"So what?"

"You can't kill ladybugs," said Oliver. "It's bad karma."

"A bug is a bug," said Tobias.

"Not true. There are a gazillion different types," I said. "And ladybugs are too cute to smush."

"Exactly," said Oliver.

Not every guy would defend the life of a ladybug so zealously, and for that I was grateful. But still wary. I stood up and moved closer for two reasons. One, I wanted to check it out. And two, I felt like I needed to protect the bug from Tobias.

Its shell was more orange than red. Because it didn't move at all it looked dead, but I sensed it was still alive. Maybe it was injured or maybe it had frozen in fear, too scared to fly away. It sure had reason to be. Just moments ago it had almost been smashed. Not that its little bug brain could comprehend that fact. Or maybe it could. What did I know about bug brains? Nothing!

"Here," I said, and rested my pointer finger on Oliver's arm. "Come on, little guy."

"It's a ladybug. Not a guy," said Tobias.

"Figure of speech," I said, keeping my finger still.

"And I'm sure there are male ladybugs," Oliver said. He kept his arm up and eventually the bug crawled onto my finger, tickling it ever so slightly.

I carefully raised my finger to Oliver's lips. "Ladybug elevator going up!" I said, then felt embarrassed for cracking such a silly joke.

Tobias rolled his eyes but Oliver actually giggled.

"Okay, make a wish," I said.

He grinned, closed his eyes, and blew.

"What'd you wish for?" I asked, even though I know you're not supposed to share.

"A first prize idea," said Oliver.

"You guys are too corny," Tobias said with a grumble.

"That's it!" said Oliver, opening his eyes.

"Corn?" I asked.

"No, we should do something related to bugs. Unless you're allergic, Tobias."

I stifled a laugh because I didn't want to upset Tobias. Not when we needed him to agree with us.

Because the more I thought about it, the more brilliant it sounded. No one else I knew had even considered studying bugs. And they were everywhere, so we'd have no trouble finding some to study.

Oliver's cheeks flushed with the pride of knowing he'd come up with it—the perfect science fair project. Or at least the beginning of one . . .

I took a deep breath and glanced at Tobias. Here's the crazy thing—he was smiling, too.

"That actually sounds cool," he said. "As long as we find the right experiment."

"Which won't involve dissecting," Oliver said.

"Or harming bugs in any way, shape, or form," I added.

"I know!" said Tobias. "You guys should give me a little more credit." He picked up one of the books and began flipping through the pages. Oliver read over his shoulder, so I looked down at the second book.

"Are backyard bugs color blind?" Oliver said a few moments later. "And if not, what colors do they prefer?"

I held my breath. This wasn't just a great idea. It was our only idea.

"We could totally do this," said Tobias. "And I like bugs."

"I do, too," I whispered.

Oliver grinned at me. "So it's settled."

"Awesome! See you nerds later!" Tobias slapped Oliver five and then me, and then he was gone. It was all I could do not to sigh in relief.

"I guess I should get going, too," I said, looking toward the house.

"If you have to," said Oliver. "Or we can play some Nerf basketball—'cause you sure could use the practice!"

## chapter six
### dates

**W**hy are you smiling so much when Yumi is perpetually late?" Rachel asked me the next morning.

"Per-what?" I asked.

"*Perpetual* is today's word. It's a fancier way of saying indefinitely, which is a fancier way of saying for a long, long time."

"Maybe we're perpetually early," I said. "And you're perpetually stressed out for no good reason."

"Okay, fine, but that still doesn't explain your chipper mood."

"Whenever someone says *chipper* I think of chipmunks, which is funny because chipmunks aren't exactly chipper animals, you know?"

I didn't answer Rachel directly because I didn't want her to know that I was thinking about yesterday afternoon at Oliver's. How after Tobias left, we'd played three rounds of Nerf basketball. Then he tried to explain the rules of cricket. Apparently it's just like baseball but totally different. The game has two innings, not nine. Players hit with a paddle rather than a bat. And the ball is smaller and harder than a regular baseball. Also? It's red with white stitching instead of white with red stitching.

I had so much fun, I didn't even mind that Tobias was on our team. Okay, we didn't have Emma's brain-power, which meant we'd have to work extra hard and get super-lucky to win first place, but there was always a chance—and at least we'd have fun.

Rachel looked off in the distance and stomped her foot. "I can't believe she's not here yet!"

"Are you that excited about getting to school?" I asked.

"No," said Rachel. "I mean yes. Kind of. The thing is—I have big news. It's dance related and I need to wait for Yumi so I don't have to explain twice."

Just then I wondered if I'd forgotten my math homework. I remembered doing it but not packing it, so I opened up my backpack and pulled out my note-book. Phew! It was all there.

Rachel stared at me. "Don't you want to hear the news?"

"You mean now?" I zipped my backpack closed once more but left it at my feet, since it was heavy and who knew when Yumi would show. "Sure."

"I'm going to go with Caleb O'Conner."

"Who?"

Rachel retied her ponytail. "I keep forgetting that you're new and don't know everyone. But you must've seen Caleb. He dresses like one of the surfer dudes and he's got shaggy dark hair that always hangs in his eyes and he's kind of short."

"You just described half the boys in our grade," I pointed out.

"I know, but Caleb is the only one who wears tan Ugg boots every single day—even with shorts."

"You mean Jean-Claude?" I asked.

"Huh?"

"He's in my French class and we only use French names."

"That must be him," said Rachel. "He definitely takes French."

"He's cute!" I said.

"His ears stick out too much," said Rachel. "But yeah, he's cute."

"And his accent is very authentic-sounding. That's what our teacher says, anyway. But I thought you were holding out for Erik."

"I was but the dance is less than four weeks away and I can't wait forever. Anyway, I heard that Erik and Hannah were holding hands at the mall last week-end."

"Whoa."

"Exactly," said Rachel. "So I needed a new plan. And luckily, Caleb saw Claire after school yesterday and he asked her if I had a date yet and she said no. And then he asked her to ask me if I'd be interested in going with him and I told her yes. So now she just has to relay the message." Rachel checked her watch.

"Something that should happen this morning. Which means that if all goes well, I'll have a date by lunch-time."

"Amazing!" I felt excited for Rachel, but a little worried, too. What if everyone lined up dates before I even figured out whom I wanted to go with? There'd be no guys left.

"Do you think there are more boys or girls in our grade?" I wondered.

"Why do you ask?" Yumi said, sneaking up behind us.

Rachel spun around and yelled, "Finally!"

Yumi scrunched her eyebrows together. "What do you mean? I'm totally early today."

"She's got news," I explained.

"You mean about Caleb?" asked Yumi.

"You already know?" Rachel cried.

"Yup. I was at Claire's yesterday. You know, for the science fair thing, and she told me. Congratulations."

"Thanks," said Rachel.

"Did you guys find a good topic?" I asked.

"Yeah. We're growing plants under—"

Just then Yumi's phone pinged with a new text message. She looked down at it and smiled.

"Who's that?" I asked.

"No one," said Yumi.

"No one?" asked Rachel.

"Um, just my mom." Yumi pocketed her phone. "We should get going, right?"

"Sure." Rachel looked at me with raised eyebrows.

She didn't have to say anything else because we were obviously thinking the very same thing. Yumi texted all the time these days. And something told us it wasn't with her mother.

## chapter seven
### bugs r us

Oliver's mom picked up me and Tobias and Oliver from school on Friday and took us to Target so we could stock up on supplies for our experiment. Then as soon as we got back to his house we started setting everything up in the backyard.

"Something about getting brand-new stuff for a brand-new project is pretty cool," said Oliver, tearing open a fresh pack of multicolored construction paper.

"I was just thinking that," I said. "It's like anything is possible. We might win first prize and we might even turn in the best science fair project in the entire history of Birchwood Middle School."

"Yeah." Oliver smiled. "Or maybe we'll make an important discovery in the field of entomology. That's the fancy way of saying 'the study of bugs.' I looked it up last night."

"Or we might fail miserably," said Tobias.

Oliver and I both glared at him.

"What?" He threw up his hands. "It's possible. I mean, I don't really think that'll happen, but it had to be said."

"It didn't *have* to be said," I replied.

"Anyway, I thought I could design a cool cover for the report, like with bugs crawling out of the word *entomology*," said Oliver.

"You could do that?" I asked.

Oliver nodded. "My art teacher said we could focus on the anatomy of the ant during our next couple of sessions."

"I thought you took stained glass," I said.

"I do," said Oliver. "I mean my private art teacher. I've been taking lessons for a couple of years."

"That's so cool," I said.

"Know what else would be cool?" said Tobias. "If you two quit jibber jabbering so we could get to work."

"Jibber jabbering?" I asked. "Really?"

"Let's just start," said Oliver. "According to the instructions, we're supposed to place six pieces of construction paper on the lawn—each one a different color. And then we just sit back and watch where bugs land."

"Watch and record so we can compare the data later," said Tobias. "I think we should do that for two hours at a time. That way we'll get a good sample."

"Sounds good to me," I said.

After some debate over colors, we chose red, blue, yellow, white, black, and green. Then we set them out on the grass. Tobias drew a diagram of the lawn and measured the space between each page so we could reproduce the same conditions every time.

Once he finished, we all sat down in the grass and stared at the paper.

We were searching for patterns. Did certain types of bugs prefer certain colors? If so, which bugs and which colors? Inquiring minds wanted to know—at least at first.

Nothing happened for a while. Then nothing happened some more. Finally a fly landed on the red sheet.

"There's a fly!" said Oliver.

"Duh," said Tobias, making a mark on the first page of our brand-new notebook.

A few seconds later it flew off and then a roly-poly bug crawled onto the yellow sheet. Next a bee buzzed over to the blue sheet, stopped for a moment, and then moved on.

After about fifteen minutes and a bunch more bug activity, I realized something. "Know what?" I asked.

"Watching bugs is kinda boring," said Oliver.

"Um, yeah!" I laughed. "Maybe we should just observe for half an hour at a time. I mean, no one said we had to do this for two hours, right?"

"That's the best idea I've heard all day," said Oliver.

"You two are so cute," Tobias said in this weird tone of voice, like he was making fun of us except I didn't get the joke. Not exactly, anyway.

"Shut up, dude," said Oliver.

"Defending your girlfriend?" asked Tobias. "You're too much."

Just then Oliver tackled Tobias.

Tobias laughed as the two of them wrestled—their bodies tumbling across the lawn, right over our experiment.

"Hey, cut it out! Be careful!" I yelled. But they ignored me. "You're gonna crush the bugs!"

When they finally broke it up, all of our construction paper was wrinkled, and the yellow and green pieces were ripped.

"Aaargh! Now we have to start over!" I said.

"No biggie," Oliver said with a shrug. "There's plenty of paper."

Tobias straightened his glasses. "He started it."

"I don't care," I said. "Let's just do this."

We set out the paper again and sat down, and this time we were all business. No one said a word that wasn't related to bug activity. After thirty minutes we picked up the paper, shook off the bugs, and put it away.

Then we had some more ginger cookies and compared our notes.

"I think we need to mention the few bugs that landed on our paper before you guys got into a fight, because Ms. Roberts says we have to keep track of everything—even when things go wrong. That's the only way to get accurate results."

"But Tobias's lameness has nothing to do with our project," said Oliver. "And we started over."

"I think your girlfriend is right," said Tobias. "We can't start over every time we don't like what happened."

"I'm choosing to ignore you," said Oliver.

"About the project or your girlfriend?" asked Tobias.

Omigosh—this was so embarrassing.

"No comment," said Oliver.

Tobias grinned. "But you're talking to me, and if you're talking to me you're acknowledging me, which means you're not ignoring me. Nor are you denying what I just said."

"Shut up!" said Oliver.

"Don't fight!" I said. "You guys are wasting time."

"Okay, but I really think it's okay to start from scratch," said Oliver.

"Let me look it up," said Tobias, reaching for Oliver's laptop.

I took another ginger cookie and stole a glance at Oliver. He rolled his eyes as if to say, "Tobias is ridiculous."

I smiled at him with one side of my mouth.

"Hey, check this out," Tobias said, spinning the laptop around so we could read the screen. "Remember how Ms. Roberts talked about those websites where you could buy projects?"

"Yup." I nodded.

"Here's one of the sites."

We looked at the screen, which read SCIENCE FAIR PROJECT SAMPLES, $49.99. EVERYTHING YOU NEED FOR A WINNING PROJECT.

"That's just some site selling supplies," I said.

Tobias shook his head. "No, that's what they advertise, but they're really about selling entire projects. Check it out. There's stuff on light, on the solar system, on—this one's cool. It's on animals' sense of smell, and they send you models of different animal noses carved out of soapstone."

"Are you sure they sell whole projects?" asked Oliver. "That's crazy!"

Tobias nodded. "Apparently some girl at Birchwood bought one of them last year and totally got busted."

"Who?" asked Oliver.

"Someone my brother knows. He said she got suspended for two weeks."

"Whoa," said Oliver.

"Yeah—but I didn't even tell you the worst part. She actually never came back to school."

"What do you mean?" I asked.

"I mean she just disappeared. Rumor has it her parents sent her to reform school, but nobody knows for sure."

Suddenly I got the shivers. Even just looking at the website made me feel guilty, although I hadn't done anything wrong.

Oliver reached over and closed the laptop. "Know what—we shouldn't even be looking at this. What if someone accuses us and they, like, confiscate my laptop and find out we've been on these sites?"

"You watch too many crime shows," said Tobias.

"Maybe," said Oliver. "But I don't want to accidentally plagiarize or anything. Let's just agree not to go to that site ever again."

"Fine with me," said Tobias.

"Me, too," I said. I had the same fear—that I'd accidentally copy something illegally. It's just that I was too shy to admit it out loud. That Oliver had, well, it impressed me.

I looked at Oliver. He was going over our notes intently, not noticing me at all, and I couldn't help but stare.

Then suddenly he looked up and grinned. If Tobias saw he would've made fun of us, but luckily he didn't.

I couldn't believe Tobias called me Oliver's girlfriend. It was so totally annoying. I mean, no way could Oliver like me. We were just friends. And yes, he was cute and sweet and, yes, we had a great time together. And okay, fine, I totally looked forward to seeing him and sometimes got shy around him and I spent an hour last night reading about his favorite cricket team, but that didn't mean I liked him. It couldn't.

Unless maybe it did.

## chapter eight
### dance plans

**W**hen we got to our lockers on Monday, I found Emma and Claire deep in conversation.

"What's up?" Rachel asked.

Emma turned to us and sighed. "Okay, it's not like it's a big deal or anything, but Phil and I are going to the dance. I mean, obviously."

"Omigosh, that's great news!" Rachel clapped little baby claps and let out the kind of squeal I last heard from the dolphin tank at SeaWorld.

"I guess." Emma's shoulders seemed kind of slumpy and not at all like shoulders that just got invited to their first school dance.

"What's wrong?" I asked.

"It's the way he asked her," Claire explained.

"What do you mean?" Rachel wondered.

Emma sighed. "He was bragging about his science fair project last night on the phone and he made a joke about how we could celebrate his victory at the dance."

"He's that sure he's going to win?" I asked. "What's he doing?"

"I can't tell you because he swore me to secrecy," said Emma.

"But we're your best friends," said Rachel.

Emma looked around and lowered her voice. "Okay, promise you won't say anything? Because he made me swear not to tell anyone."

"I won't say a word," I promised.

"And neither will I," said Yumi.

"He's building a maze for his hamster, but that's just the beginning. He has this whole theory about sports and nutrition. He thinks that junk food gets a bad rap. That candy is a better motivator and that a short-term sugar high is more effective for sprinters than any green vegetable. So it's Snickers versus broccoli. Basically, he's trying to figure out whether Einstein is more motivated by junk food or health food."

"I know what I'd rather have," I said.

"Me, too," said Emma. "And there are certain marathon runners who eat junk food before a big race, thinking that calories are calories and it doesn't matter where they come from. Quality does not matter. Strict caloric intake is all that counts."

"Sounds cool," Claire said.

"Or boring." Rachel turned to Emma. "So what are you going to wear?"

"To the science fair?" she asked.

"No, dummy. To the dance!"

"A dress, I guess." Emma shrugged.

"And high heels?" asked Rachel.

73

"I don't have any."

"That doesn't mean you can't buy any."

"If I can't walk in heels, it's going to be hard to dance in them," said Emma.

"Good point," said Rachel. "Maybe heels are too dressy, anyway. It's not a formal dance. Just a regular dance dance."

"What does that even mean?" Emma asked.

"It means that you can wear a skirt or a casual dress but nothing too shiny," said Claire. "Unless it's like a sparkly top paired with something more casual, like jeans or tight black pants. Or shiny pants with a muted sweater."

"You're sure?" asked Rachel.

Claire nodded. "I've already checked with Charlie and Olivia, and they pretty much told me that anything goes. There's always one or two people who get decked out and go formal, but mostly it's guys in jeans and shirts with collars or khakis and T-shirts. Not too many people wear khakis and a collared shirt. Some guys goof and wear ties, but only ironically. Usually they pair them with old jeans or shorts. And as for girls, some of them get their hair and nails done and buy new outfits, while others act super-casual about the whole thing—like it's no biggie and they go to dances every weekend."

Charlie and Olivia are Claire's twin brother and sister, eighth graders and our secret expert consultants on all things related to middle school. So we listened intently. Although this particular advice was hard to follow.

"Do you think it's cooler to be fancy or to go casual?" asked Emma.

"I don't know how much it matters, as long as you have a date," said Rachel. "Which reminds me—you guys need to work on that."

I gulped. She was right. But at least now I knew who I wanted to go with. All I had to do was figure out how to make it happen.

## chapter nine
### kissing action

**Y**umi turned twelve on Saturday and the five of us went to Fun-A-Palooza for her birthday. That's this really cool sports complex with go-carts, miniature golf, batting cages, and a huge arcade with all the best games.

Last time I went, my mom made me choose between racing on the go-cart track and hitting at the batting cages, and I chose the go carts, obviously. But for Yumi's party we didn't have to choose. We were staying all day, which meant we'd get to do it all.

Besides being super-excited about the party and hanging out with my friends, I was also glad I'd finally get the opportunity to talk to everyone about Oliver.

I'd had a crush on him for almost an entire week and I hadn't told anyone.

Not even my diary.

Of course, I don't tell my diary anything. My mom gave it to me on my tenth birthday and I haven't written in it since the day I opened it. And even then all I wrote was, "Dear Diary, Today is my birthday and my mom got me this journal."

Guess I've had a serious case of writer's block ever since.

Anyway, I couldn't talk about Oliver at school because I didn't want anyone to overhear and spread rumors. The last thing I needed was to be gossiped about at Birchwood Middle School.

And I still hadn't figured out whether or not I should bring up my crush in the first place.

Not before I asked Oliver to the dance.

If I was going to ask him.

Of course, that posed yet another problem, because what if I did ask him and he said no? Things might get awkward and we still had to work together for two weeks and six days. And that's just counting our science fair project. Even if I did manage to survive that weirdness, he'd still be my lab partner until school got out. And that was months away.

On the other hand, what if Oliver did like me and he was simply too shy to say so? Maybe he's been dying to ask me to the dance for weeks and hasn't been able to bring himself to make a move. Not to sound full of myself or completely delusional, because there were some signs.

At least I think there were. When we first started going to his house to work on our bug project, he asked if I wanted iced tea or lemonade and I said half-and-half. Then, on the second meeting he said, "Half-and-half, right, Annabelle?" And on the third meeting, and every meeting since then, he hasn't even had to ask. He just pours me a half-and-half automatically.

Remembering my favorite drink has got to count for something.

Or maybe I was just looking too hard. Oliver also remembered that Tobias liked lemonade. So maybe Oliver is just a nice guy with a really good memory.

But even forgetting the drinks, I had other reasons to be suspicious.

Oliver defended me whenever Tobias made rude comments, and that happened all the time. Of course, any good friend would defend me.

And I did catch him staring at me yesterday. True, I'd had a spinach calzone for lunch. So it's entirely possible that I had something green stuck in my teeth and didn't realize it. Maybe Oliver wanted to say something but decided not to because he didn't want to embarrass me.

I checked my teeth when I got home and didn't see anything. But maybe it had been there at Oliver's and only got dislodged on my way home. It's a five-minute drive, which by any calculation is plenty of time for a measly piece of spinach to dislodge and disappear.

Maybe I just wanted Oliver to stare at me so desperately that I convinced myself he had been when really he was staring at something just over my shoulder, like one of his mom's watercolors of the sea. They were really pretty. But he could stare at his mom's paintings anytime. Why do so when I was standing in his way?

Obviously I felt seriously confused. I needed advice, which is where my friends came in.

But I didn't bring Oliver up while we were at the batting cages. Someone was always hitting, and I didn't want to have to repeat the information twice.

Plus, the machines were loud and I didn't want to shout.

Being in the arcade posed the same problem. And I couldn't say anything when we were in the middle of the go-cart races. . . .

Even when we went out for pizza afterward, I couldn't tell them because Yumi's parents were at our table, and her baby sister, Suki, and her grandma. (Not the one who lives in Hawaii.)

Mrs. Tamagachi seemed sweet and all, but no way was I going to talk about liking a boy in front of someone's grandma. It's just not done.

After lunch and then another hour at the arcade, we headed back to Yumi's for a "make your own party hat" craft, then a "make your own sushi" dinner and then a "make your own sundae" dessert, followed by a "make your own sleepover."

By the time we'd rolled out our sleeping bags, I figured I'd waited long enough. Not only was I exhausted from making so much stuff, I also knew that if I didn't say something tonight, I'd never get the chance to. But for some reason, I kept stalling.

The timing never seemed right. Not even after Rachel brought up the school dance. "Two weeks and counting until Valentine's Day," she said, looking at her watch. "Ticktock."

"Digital watches don't make that sound," said Emma.

Rachel whacked her in the head with a pillow. "It's a figure of speech, smarty-pants."

Emma laughed. "I never understood that expression—smarty-pants. How can pants be smart? Or legs, even?"

Everyone groaned, and justifiably so.

Then Rachel started up again. "You guys, this is serious. We need to make plans."

"Easy for you to say. You've already got a date," said Claire.

"I know," Rachel said. "I just wish it was with Erik. Or at least with someone who was more like Erik. Like his secret twin."

"Erik has a secret twin?" I asked.

"Only in her dreams," said Emma.

Rachel turned to me and asked, "Has he asked Hannah to the dance yet?"

"Not sure," I said, which was technically true. I didn't tell Rachel that when our other classmate, Becky, asked Hannah about the dance, Hannah had changed the subject fast, without answering her.

"You should be happy you have a date," said Claire. "Looks like I'll be going solo, unless Yumi lends me one of her dates."

"What?" Rachel and I asked at the same time.

Yumi blushed. "I kind of got asked."

"By two guys," said Claire.

"And you didn't tell us?" asked Emma.

Yumi took off her party hat and tossed it aside. "It seemed too braggy to mention and I don't know what to do."

"Well, who asked you?" asked Rachel.

"Dante and Ezra," Yumi said.

I felt a stab of envy, even though I didn't know who either of these guys were. "I can't believe you have two dates."

"No, I've got none," said Yumi. "Yes, they both asked me, but I haven't given either one of them answers."

"So which one do you like?" asked Rachel.

"Neither." Yumi shrugged. "I mean, they're both nice. Dante is a better baseball player, but Ezra is really funny. And not just gross armpit-fart funny or check-out-how-far-I-can-shoot-a-spitball hilarious. He's much more sophisticated."

"Too bad you can't go with both of them," said Claire.

"Well, *technically* you can," said Rachel. "The dance will be crowded and it's not like they're even friends. So you could agree to meet them both there and just make sure they stay on opposite sides of the gym. Then you can run back and forth between songs, maybe changing dresses with each guy."

"Why would I have to change dresses?" asked Yumi.

"I don't know," said Rachel. "Maybe to match each corsage?"

Yumi shook her head. "That sounds like a night-mare."

"Or an old *Brady Bunch* episode," I said.

"Oh yeah." Rachel blushed.

"Anyway, wouldn't her dates both want to escort her to the dance?" I asked.

"Look at you, all formal," said Claire. "Escort!"

Everyone giggled.

"What's so funny?" I asked.

"That's not how it works in junior high," Rachel explained. "Everyone just goes to the dances with their friends and they meet their dates there."

"It all changes in high school," Claire added.

"But I don't think I want to go with either guy," said Yumi. "And it seems wrong to say yes just so I'll have a date. Almost like I was using one of them and—" Yumi stopped talking because her phone chimed with a new text message.

She reached for it, but Rachel got there first.

"What are you—hey stop!" Yumi cried, lunging for her phone, but Rachel wouldn't let go. In fact, she stood up on her tippy-toes and held it over her head, far from Yumi's grasp.

"That's private property!" Yumi yelled.

"I'll give it back to you as soon as you tell us who you've been texting all this time!"

"Okay, fine, but this is so mean to do to me on my birthday!"

"I'm doing it because I care!" Rachel said as she

handed back Yumi's phone. I kind of wished she'd read her text first. Forget that it's an invasion of privacy—I was curious. We all were.

"Don't keep us in suspense!" I said.

"I said I'd tell you." Yumi brushed her hair from her face. "I met a boy in Hawaii."

"What?" Claire asked.

"That's so great!" said Emma.

"And you're just telling us now?" asked Rachel.

"You never asked," Yumi said.

"That's the kind of information you're just supposed to volunteer," Rachel said.

"So what's his name?" I asked.

"Nathan," Yumi said.

"Have any pictures?" asked Emma.

"Of course. Hold on. Let me just write him back." Yumi began texting.

"What did he write?" asked Rachel.

"Wait a sec." Once Yumi finished, she looked up at us and smiled. "Just Happy Birthday. Surf's up!"

"Surf's up?" asked Rachel.

"It's an inside joke," said Yumi. "Too complicated to explain. You had to be there."

"And what are you writing back?" asked Rachel.

"None of your business!" said Yumi. After she finished, she brought up a tiny picture on her cell phone screen.

We all huddled around the phone, trying to make out the image. The sun glinted in the background, making it hard to see his face, and her screen was tiny. Almost too tiny for the five of us to be looking at once, but we managed.

Nathan seemed cute. He wore a green and blue floral print bathing suit and a blue and white rash guard. He was standing on the beach. He had black hair, or maybe it just looked that way because it was wet.

"Let's see." Claire moved in closer.

Rachel took the phone.

"Careful not to delete him!" said Yumi.

"Don't worry!" said Rachel. "I have my own phone, so it's not like I don't know what I'm doing."

When the phone finally got passed to me, I quickly scrolled through the shots. There were four pictures— the original of Nathan standing on the beach. Then Nathan biting into a hamburger, Nathan holding a boogie board, and Nathan smiling and waving at the camera.

None of Yumi and Nathan holding hands or riding horses together on the beach or having a picnic—those are the romantic images that flashed through my mind when Yumi first said she'd met a boy in Hawaii. But I guess if they were both doing all those things together it would be hard to document themselves on film. It's not like they could hire a photographer.

"How'd you meet him?" I asked, handing back the phone.

"And where does he live?" Rachel asked.

"Did you guys kiss?" Claire wondered.

"Shh! Keep it down." Yumi glanced at the door. "My parents are in the next room!"

"You mean they don't know about him?" Rachel gasped. "Is it forbidden love?"

"No. Of course my parents know him," said Yumi. "Our grandmas are friends, and his lives in the condo complex next door to mine. But they don't want me spending too much time talking to him. Right now, I can only call him on weekends, after I finish all my homework. Luckily they never said anything about texting. . . ."

"So that's why you've been spending so much time staring at your phone!" said Claire.

Yumi didn't deny this. In fact, she didn't say a word. I couldn't believe she'd been sitting on the news for so long—acting like everything was normal when she was involved in a secret romance! For weeks now!

"So what's the story? Tell us everything," I said.

Yumi tiptoed to the doorway and peered out. "Okay, the coast is clear," she said, joining us on the floor again. "We met on my third day there. That's when his family arrived. They live in Michigan."

"Michigan? That's so far away," said Claire.

"It's in the Midwest," Yumi told us. "In a different time zone, even."

"So that's why you don't want to go to the dance with any guy from Birchwood," said Rachel. "Because you have a secret boyfriend who lives far away."

Yumi shook her head. "No, we're not going out. We both know that it would be pointless because who knows if we'll ever get to see each other again?"

"But that's why you want to spend the summer in Hawaii," said Emma.

"Well, yeah," said Yumi. "He's trying to do the same thing, so we can be together, but I don't think it's going to work. And I know summer is far away but I can't stop thinking about him."

"Did you kiss him?" asked Claire.

Yumi nodded and we all screamed into our pillows.

"Keep it down!" Yumi said, eyes wide and arms waving. "My parents don't know about that part—obviously. Although I think they caught us holding hands once. So embarrassing."

"What was it like?" asked Emma.

"Amazing," said Yumi. "Magical. You know."

"I know," said Emma. "That's how it was the first time with me. And that was just in my backyard. You guys were in Hawaii. On the beach."

"Actually, we were at a snow cone stand." Yumi tucked her hair behind her ears and smiled. "Well, the parking lot of the snow cone stand."

"Did it happen before or after you ate snow cones?" asked Rachel.

"Before we finished eating, but after we ordered."

"What kind of snow cones were they?" asked Claire.

"Like it matters!" said Rachel.

"Of course it matters. It's her first kiss. Everything

matters." Claire turned back to Yumi. "We need all the details."

"I had cherry and blue raspberry. He had cola and coconut."

"Did you taste his snow cone on your lips?" asked Rachel.

Yumi made her nose-crinkle face. "Not really. Luckily. I think coconut is gross."

"I can't believe you kissed a boy and never even told us about it," said Claire.

"Shh!" Yumi raised a finger to her lips and gestured toward the door. "Parents. Right outside."

"Sorry," said Claire. "I'm just excited for you, is all. Anyway, I told you when I had my first kiss."

"Wait, you did? How did I miss that?" I asked.

"It happened before we knew you," said Claire.

"So fill me in!" I hardly believed all this news. I was seeing a whole new side of my friends. Were they always this mature and grown-up? And if so, how come I never noticed before?

Claire grinned. "It happened last summer, but I'm not even sure if it counts because it was a spin-the-bottle kiss at my cousin's birthday party up in Fresno."

"We've been over this," said Rachel. "Your lips touched, so it definitely counts."

"It's true," said Yumi. "A kiss is a kiss."

"So what was it like?" I asked.

"Fast," she said. "Faster than a blink almost. And I felt it on my lips and in my stomach. Kind of like a hiccup, but a really fun one. I was so embarrassed, but the guys seemed to be, too, so that made me feel better. Like, I didn't have to worry about doing it wrong."

"How would you do it wrong?" Rachel asked, giggling.

"My point is, I knew I'd never have to see them again. So the pressure was off."

"Were they cute?" I asked.

"One was very cute and one was okay," said Claire. "Although the really cute guy had bad breath. And the only so-so one had really soft lips. He was the better kisser, I think, of the two, anyway. It's not like I have vast amounts of experience."

"Have you ever kissed anyone?" Claire asked.

"Who me?" I asked, even though Claire—and everyone else—was looking my way, so it was pretty obvious. "Um, not really. I mean, no. Never. Not yet, that is. I used to go to an all-girls school, remember? Even my camp was just for girls."

"It'll happen," Claire said with confidence.

Suddenly I felt really, really young. Like someone's little sister tagging along at the big kids' party.

"Rachel hasn't kissed anyone yet, either," said Yumi.

"Rub it in, why don't you." Rachel turned to Yumi. "But let's not talk about my pathetic lack of a love life."

"Says the girl who Caleb is madly in love with," Claire said.

"He's not in love with me," said Rachel.

"He drew your initials on his jeans," said Claire.

"Those could've been anyone's initials," said Rachel. "Tell us more about Nathan."

"But first tell us more about the kissing," Claire said, and the rest of us giggled.

"Did you do it a lot?" asked Claire.

Yumi nodded. "After the first six times, I stopped counting."

"Wow!" said Emma. "You've probably kissed more than me."

"But you've kissed two boys, for real," said Yumi. "No offense, Claire."

"None taken," Claire replied.

She was referring to Emma's ex-boyfriend, Corn Dog Joe, and her current boyfriend, Phil.

Emma shook her head. "Actually, Phil and I haven't kissed yet. We've just held hands. A lot."

"How come?" asked Yumi.

Emma shrugged. "Maybe he's waiting until Valentine's Day?"

"I'm glad you brought that up," said Rachel. "Yumi, I understand that you're into this dude, but you should still go to the dance. Just choose one of them and if you can't decide then flip a coin."

"I can't do that!" said Yumi.

"Sure you can. It's easy." Rachel fished a quarter out of her backpack. "I'll do it. Heads is Dante, tails is Ezra, okay?"

Yumi nodded and Rachel tossed the coin in the air. It landed on its side and rolled into a corner.

We all ran over to see what the verdict was. Heads.

"Does that still count?" asked Claire.

"Sure," I said.

"Dante it is," said Rachel.

"But I don't want him to think I like him," said Yumi.

"Just tell him you can only go to the dance as friends because your heart belongs to a boy in Michigan," Rachel said.

"That's so corny!" said Yumi.

"But it's the truth," said Rachel. "And there's no reason that you should sit home alone on a Saturday night when you could be out having fun. Think of Dante as your backup date. He's your Caleb."

Yumi shook her head. "But I won't have to be alone. Nathan and I can have a texting date. Or we can IM. And I'm trying to convince my parents to get me a new computer so we can do a video chat. My old one keeps crashing every time I try and download the software."

"It's not cool to stay home all night staring at a computer," said Emma.

"Even if there's a super-cute boy to talk to?" asked Yumi.

"Even so. You need to get out! If you don't want to bring a date, I understand. But you should at least come to the dance."

Yumi twisted up her mouth like she was thinking really hard. "I guess I'll consider it."

"Good!" said Rachel. "So that just leaves Anna-belle and Claire. How goes Operation Find-a-Date?"

I opened my mouth, trying to figure out the best way to bring up Oliver. But before I managed to get a word in, Claire said, "Guess what? I like someone. Although *like* is too mild a term. Basically, I'm madly in love with him and I'm pretty sure he likes me back," she said.

"That's great! Who is he?" I asked.

Claire grinned, her blue eyes gleaming. "Oliver."

## chapter ten
### not *that* oliver ...

**E**ver get soaked by a surprise water balloon? Stub your toe? Or bang your funny bone on the corner of a table?

That's what it felt like in those first few moments after Claire told everyone she liked Oliver: stunning, sharp, and painful.

Then I had a hopeful thought. Maybe Claire was referring to an entirely different Oliver. It's a common name. There must be hundreds of them at school.

Okay maybe not hundreds. But there had to be others. One other. All I needed was one.

I racked my brain in search of another boy named Oliver, and that's when it came to me—there's an eighth grader named Oliver and I think he's friends with Claire's big brother, Charlie. Yes, he must be. He's probably at their house all the time, which is how come Claire noticed him.

I felt the knot in my stomach begin to unravel.

At least until Rachel said, "He does have a great accent and he's so cute."

"What kind of accent?" I asked, still clinging to the slight possibility that there could be a second Oliver from an entirely different country.

"Jamaican, obviously." Claire shot me a funny look. "You know that."

"You don't mean Oliver Banks!" I blurted out.

"Of course him. Who else?"

"Uh, doesn't your brother have a friend named Oliver?" I asked.

"Nope," said Claire. "I don't even think there's any other Oliver at Birchwood."

Great, now I was imagining things! I giggled out of nervousness. "Oh, sorry. I must be thinking of someone at my old school."

"But you didn't have any boys at your old school," said Rachel.

I forced another laugh to mask the sound of my splintering heart. "Um, oh yeah. I forgot."

"Do you guys have any classes together?" asked Yumi.

"Just lunch, if that counts." Claire smiled and sat up straighter, like just talking about Oliver—my Oliver—put her in a bright and shiny mood. "I always thought he was cute, but I ran into him at the mall right after Christmas and we hung out."

"You hung out?" I hoped my friends didn't notice the nervous tremor in my voice.

"Kind of. We said hi, anyway. And I asked him how his Christmas was and he said, 'Great. Just got back from Jamaica.' And I said, 'Lucky you,' and he smiled, and then as he was leaving he said, 'Have a good one,' and sort of saluted."

"Wow," said Yumi.

Okay, now I felt like I'd been punched in the stomach.

True, no one's ever actually punched me in the stomach, but it had to be better than hearing Claire go on and on and on about my crush.

Oliver had never—not once—kind of saluted to me.

He smiled at me a lot. He taught me how to swing a cricket bat. And last time I was at his house he showed me his portfolio. Besides sketching bugs, he likes painting pictures of his favorite waterfall in Jamaica. He also has one very lifelike picture of his swimming pool. It's inspired by an artist named David Hockney, he said. And when I told him I'd never heard of David Hockney, Oliver said not to worry about it. He hadn't, either, until his dad took him to an exhibit in the city last summer.

My point being, we had real conversations about meaningful stuff. Wasn't that better than a kind of salute? I didn't ask out loud because it seemed rude, but I did wonder.

And once I stopped wondering, I started wishing I'd spoken up thirty seconds sooner because if I had, my friends would be talking about *my* crush on Oliver, not Claire's. But now it was too late. There was no turning back.

"You have to wonder about his taste, though," said Rachel. "Since he used to go out with one of the Three Terrors."

"He and Jesse broke up weeks ago. During winter break," I reminded her.

"Right, so he's been single for ages," said Yumi.

"And everyone makes mistakes," Claire said with a grin.

"Is it true his mom used to be a model?" asked Yumi.

"She paints," I said. "Really pretty watercolors. And Oliver is into art, too, except he likes working with oils and he's also good at drawing. He takes private classes and he visits museums in the city."

Claire stared at me, her head tilted to one side like she was trying to figure something out. I know that look because Pepper gives it to me whenever he suspects I have food. Except something told me Claire wasn't hungry. Not in the conventional sense, that is, so I decided it would be a good time to stop talking.

"Are you going to ask him to the dance, or try and get him to ask you?" asked Rachel.

This made my heart sink to depths I didn't know existed.

As my friends peppered Claire with questions, I wondered, how did this work? Like, what were the rules? Could we both like Oliver? I mean, we both did, but should I admit it, too? It seemed wrong to just blurt it out. Too late, at least. But was it really?

Claire would be upset if I told everyone about my crush—I knew she would. But did she have a right to be?

And what about Oliver? Just because Claire liked him didn't necessarily mean he had to like her back. I'm sure he had an opinion. So maybe we could ask him to choose between us? No, that would be wrong. Weird and uncomfortable, like some dumb reality show: *Help! My best friend and I are crushing on the same boy!*

The longer I waited to say something, the worse I felt.

"I'm making all of us belts to wear to the school dance," Claire said. "In different colors so they won't be too matchy-matchy. But do you think I could make one for Oliver, too? Or would that be weird? Maybe I should make him some shoelaces instead . . ."

It was as if Claire had already called dibs on him. Like how the first person to yell "Shotgun" gets to ride in the front seat.

"How long have you been into him?" I asked, interrupting, because I couldn't stay quiet for one more second.

"Huh?" asked Claire.

"Oliver." It hurt to say his name, just to ask this question. But I really wanted—no, I needed—an answer. "How long has it been?"

"A few weeks," Claire said with a casual shrug. "I don't know the exact moment—it just sort of sneaked up on me."

Unfortunately, I knew exactly how she felt. And when I say exactly, I really mean EXACTLY.

I glanced down at my sleeping bag. The edges where the two zippered sides met were frayed from the fabric having gotten stuck a few too many times. I noticed a small spot of crusty old marshmallow on one corner and scraped at it with my fingernail.

"So how are you going to ask him?" Rachel wondered.

"Don't know," said Claire. "Any ideas, Annabelle?"

"Me?" I looked up. "Why would I have ideas?"

"You guys are friends, right?" she asked.

"We're lab partners." I looked down at the marshmallow mess again. "I hardly know him."

"Didn't you go to his house twice last week?" asked Rachel.

"Three times," I admitted. "But only to work on our science fair project. It doesn't mean we—"

"Are you seeing him next week, too?" Claire asked.

"Probably," I replied, not volunteering that we had plans to meet up every Monday, Wednesday, and Friday until we completed our project—and then feeling guilty for not sharing this. Like I was sneaking around behind my friend's back.

"And you sit by him in science, right?" asked Claire.

I gulped and nodded.

"So maybe you could ask him for me."

"Ask him to the dance?" I asked, horrified.

"No, silly. Just ask him *about* the dance. If he's

**97**

planning on going, if he has a date, and if he likes anyone," Claire said. "You know, if you can find a way to bring it up naturally in the conversation."

"We don't really talk about stuff like that."

"Well, what do you talk about?" Claire asked.

"Our project mostly. It's on different species of bugs and their color preferences, and sometimes we talk about cricket."

"Aren't crickets a type of bug?" asked Claire.

"No, I mean cricket the sport."

"Huh?" asked Claire.

I couldn't believe she dared crush on Oliver when she didn't even know what cricket was! "It's very popular in Jamaica. England, too. Lots of countries."

I didn't mention that I'd never heard about cricket until a few weeks ago, or that now I was an expert, having almost memorized the Wikipedia entry on the sport. That maybe would've been too revealing.

"I'm sure that in all your talk about cricket you can find a moment to bring up the dance," said Claire. "And maybe even mention my name?"

"I'll try." I forced a smile, tried really hard to put on a friendly face, but it didn't feel quite right.

For some reason, it felt more like I was baring my teeth at her.

# chapter eleven
## is a cookie just a cookie?

"Why so glum?" Ted asked me at dinner on Sunday night.

"I'm not glum. I'm Annabelle Stevens, your new stepdaughter. Remember?"

Ted laughed. "I knew you looked familiar. Thanks for clarifying."

I smirked and pushed yet another piece of chalky-looking cauliflower from one end of my plate to the other. Ted had made vegetable stir-fry—usually delicious—except tonight he'd used too much cauliflower, one of the few vegetables I can't stand, and somehow it all seemed to end up on my plate, which was actually pretty fitting since it had been a cauliflower kind of weekend.

And it's not like I could even be grateful it was almost over. School this week would be even worse. I just knew it! Now that Claire had revealed her crush, and now that I was supposed to ask the love of my life if he's interested in her.

"I'm guessing that you didn't get much sleep at Yumi's last night," Mom said.

I sighed. Mom was right, but for the wrong reasons. She probably assumed I didn't sleep because we were too busy giggling over gossip, giving each other mani-pedis, and trying to talk to ghosts with Yumi's Ouija board when in actuality my friends were all quietly in their sleeping bags by midnight. Except for Rachel, who snores, but that's not what kept me up. I'd slept through her snoring before.

Problem was, I couldn't stop obsessing over my mistake to keep my feelings for Oliver a secret for so long. What had I been thinking? And how could I force myself to stop thinking about Oliver? I had to if I was going to be a good friend to Claire. And I needed to be a good friend to Claire. She's one of the nicest people I know.

We both love animals but Claire is extraordinarily kind to them. She's been a vegetarian for over a year. I tried to stop eating meat over winter break, after Jason told me all about how cows are mistreated in the meatpacking industry. But I only lasted for three days. It was our trip to Bistro Burger that put me over the edge. They make the best bacon cheeseburgers. I don't know how Jason managed to get by with his scrawny looking portobello mushroom burger. And in truth, I felt kind of sorry for him.

Although I was still impressed with his discipline, and Claire's, too.

And another great thing about Claire? She's superpretty but she's not snobby about it at all. She's always smiling and she's nice to everyone, practically.

She's also mucho generous about sharing fashion tips and lending everyone her stuff—even her favorites.

If Oliver had to choose between us, no way would he choose me over her. And anyway, it wasn't fair to give him that choice.

Claire liked him first. Or at least she said so first. That meant she had every right to ask him to the dance. And being one of her closest friends, I had no choice but to help her out.

That's why I walked into science class on Monday with every intention of talking to Oliver about Claire.

Except I never got the chance to, because as soon as I got to class he slipped me something in a napkin.

"What's that?" I asked.

"My mom made ginger cookies over the weekend and I saved you one," said Oliver.

I unwrapped the cookie carefully, checked to make sure our teacher wasn't watching, and then took a bite. The cookie crumbled in my mouth—filling my taste buds with slightly spicy deliciousness.

"Thanks so much!"

Oliver said, "It's no biggie." But he smiled shyly, like it was a big deal or, if not that, then at least a small- to medium-size deal.

Then Tobias walked in late and smelling of pepperoni pizza. (The yucky kind from the cafeteria—not good pizza.)

I figured Oliver would give him a cookie, too, but

he didn't—maybe because class was starting or maybe because he only saved one for me.

I wondered what that meant. Good things, I was sure.

In fact, maybe if I stalled a bit, Claire would forget all about Oliver. Her crush on him seemed to spring up so suddenly. Maybe she'd lose interest just as fast. Or at least fall for someone else.

And here's a horrible thought—one that made me a lousy friend. If Claire insisted on asking Oliver, I couldn't help but secretly hope he turned her down. Not because I wanted Claire to be heartbroken. That would be terrible—the worst possible consequence. But in my heart of hearts (a phrase that doesn't make much sense to me because everyone has only one heart, as far as I know), I couldn't help but hold on to the hope that maybe—just maybe—Oliver liked someone else instead.

Someone he spent more time with.

Someone shorter. Blonder.

Someone who shared his interests: bugs, ginger cookies, Nerf basketball, lemonade mixed with iced tea, and cricket.

Someone who actually knows what cricket is (kind of).

Then I had another thought. One that wasn't too too terrible, although probably still not so nice. What if Oliver happened to ask me to the dance before I had the chance to ask him about Claire?

It could happen.

But then what if it did? Could I say yes? Or did saying yes to Oliver make me a lousy friend? What if Claire never forgave me? Even just wishing for that to happen felt lousy. But I couldn't help it.

I didn't say anything to Oliver during class. I wasn't planning to after class, either, but then I found Claire standing by my locker after school.

"What did he say?" she asked.

"Nothing," I said. "I mean I haven't asked him yet, but I'm going to his house in a few minutes."

"Perfect! You're the best, Annabelle."

Claire gave me a hug, which only made me feel worse. "Call me later and let me know how it goes," she said before taking off with a bounce in her step— like she knew I'd report back with good news.

And the thought that I'd betray her had never crossed her mind.

## chapter twelve
bugs and boys

I think the red one should be farther left," Tobias said that afternoon as we surveyed the construction paper we'd put out on Oliver's lawn.

Oliver moved the paper over ever so slightly. "How's this?" he asked.

"Let me check." Tobias pulled his tape measure from his back pocket and measured the distance from the edge of the patio. Then he compared it to our notes from last time. "No, half an inch to the right, actually."

"No problem." Oliver moved it back.

"Everything ready?" I asked.

"Wait," said Oliver. "You guys need to see my bug sketches." He opened his notebook and showed us drawings of a bumblebee, a ladybug, and an ant.

"Cool!" Tobias said.

"These are amazing!" I couldn't help but gush—because they really were. But I didn't want to say too much because I feared Tobias would make fun of me again. True, he was taking our project much more seriously lately, but I wasn't taking any chances.

"Roly-polies are next," Oliver informed us.

"Did you guys know that they're actually called armadillidiidae?" asked Tobias.

"Arma what?" I asked.

"I'll just write it down on the graph."

Once Oliver put his sketches away, I set the timer on the stopwatch for thirty minutes. "Now?" I asked.

They both nodded.

"One, two, three, go!" The second I hit the timer we all fell to the grass—not close enough to disturb, scare, or influence any bug that might land on our construction paper. But close enough so that we could actually keep track of what showed up where.

Within the first five minutes we recorded three bees, two ladybugs, six flies, and a beetle. Twenty minutes later we had an ant parade marching across the green page. And I realized I was stalling. If I didn't ask Oliver about Claire soon, I'd be out of time. And I'd promised Claire.

So I cleared my throat and blurted out the question. "Are you guys going to the school dance?"

"Dances are dumb," said Tobias.

"How do you know?" asked Oliver. "This is the first one."

"I've seen them on TV," said Tobias as he retied one of his shoelaces. "And they sound dumb."

"He's just saying that because he doesn't have a date," said Oliver.

"Do you?" I asked.

"Not yet." Oliver gave me a sideways glance. "What about you?"

"Nope." I shook my head.

"Do you want to go?" Oliver asked.

"I don't know yet," I said quickly. "My friends are, but most of them have dates. Wait. When you asked if I wanted to go did you mean—"

"You guys are too cute!" Tobias interrupted, giving Oliver a little shove. "Dude, just ask her and get it over with. Everyone knows you want to."

"Shut up!" Oliver punched Tobias in the arm.

Then Tobias hit him in the thigh. "Yo—I'm doing you a favor! If you'd just stop being such a—"

Tobias didn't get to finish his sentence because Oliver pounced on him, and the two of them went rolling across the lawn.

"Cut it out!" I screamed.

But Tobias had Oliver in a headlock and was yelling at him to say uncle, which Oliver finally did.

After Tobias let him go, Oliver stood up and brushed himself off. "That's so stupid!" he said. "Why uncle?"

"I don't know. That's just what you say," said Tobias.

"Oh, that's a good reason," Oliver said, all sarcastic.

"You guys are so immature!" I yelled.

"What?" asked Tobias. "We didn't mess up the project this time."

He was right. They'd wrestled in the opposite direction of the construction paper. But that still didn't make up for the fact that Tobias interrupted my very important question. And I couldn't bring it up again—not without humiliating myself. The moment was gone, forever. I checked my watch. "Our time is up, anyway," I said.

We recorded all the data and packed up to go home.

Except I didn't want to leave. Not when I wasn't sure about what Oliver had meant when he asked me if I wanted to go to the dance. Did he mean did I want to go with him? Or did I want to go to the dance, in general?

I hoped Oliver would invite me to stick around and watch the Lakers game with him, since we'd talked about maybe doing that in class, but now I was too embarrassed to ask—especially in front of Tobias—so I just went home.

I reported this to Claire on the phone that night. Not about how it seemed like, just possibly, Oliver might have been asking me to the dance. Just the part about how I tried to find out if Oliver was going and he didn't really answer because Tobias started teasing us.

"What do you mean, he teased you?" Claire asked.

"I think he thought Oliver wanted to go to the dance with me, which is so dumb." I forced a laugh. "I mean there's no way . . ."

I expected Claire to laugh along with me, but instead she stayed silent. I couldn't even hear her breathing on the other end of the line.

"You still there?" I asked.

"Yeah," said Claire. "Um, can I ask you something? I know this is going to sound crazy, but I was just wondering . . . you don't like Oliver, do you?"

"No way!" I shouted quickly. "Of course not. I mean I like him as a friend but that's all. Seriously. There's no way I could like him. He's way too . . ." I paused, trying to think of an excuse to give Claire. But I couldn't think of one bad thing to say about Oliver. Truth is, he wasn't too anything. "I just don't."

"Phew!" said Claire. "I'm really glad."

"Me too," I said, feeling lousy.

"So you'll try again tomorrow?"

"Oh, I won't be at his house tomorrow."

"But you have class with him," Claire said.

"Right, but obviously I can't ask him in front of Tobias again. And we're never alone together, so I just don't know how I would. Okay?"

I felt kind of bad for letting Claire down, but at the same time good that I had a reasonable excuse.

Maybe Claire would decide that asking Oliver was too complicated.

That's what I was hoping, and that's what it seemed like for a while. I didn't bring up Oliver, and Claire didn't ask me about him.

Rachel, Yumi, and I hit the mall after school a few days later to look for outfits for the dance, and Claire was supposed to come but canceled at the last minute. This I took as a good sign. Like maybe she'd decided not to bother going at all.

Yumi bought a cute black skirt and Rachel found some nice dressy black jeans. I tried on a shirtdress that they said looked good, but I didn't want to buy it.

"I don't even have a date yet," I told them as I looked at myself in the mirror. "So there's no point in buying this and it seems too dressy, anyway."

"Why don't you ask Trevor Halloway?" said Yumi.

"Who?" I asked.

"He's this cute guy in my Latin class," Yumi said.

"I hear he's going with Maya," Rachel whispered.

"See—even the guys I don't know have dates." I headed back to the dressing room.

"Sorry, you weren't supposed to hear that. But don't worry. You'll find someone," said Rachel.

*Or maybe Oliver will ask me before Claire gets around to asking him*, I thought but didn't say. That's what I was hoping would happen.

Until Friday.

## chapter thirteen
### the big shrug

I could tell something big went down by the way Claire rushed up to our table at lunch, dropped her bag down, and then sat in this extremely dramatic way. Blue eyes wide, she puffed her cheeks out like they were filled with major news.

"What's up?" I asked.

"Well," she said, "I finally talked to Oliver."

She didn't seem elated. Didn't seem happy at all, in fact.

I had a hopeful thought. Maybe Oliver turned her down. Maybe he said, "I can't go with you because my heart belongs to another girl." Or "Thanks, but it would be too complicated, a bad idea. I'm grounded. I'm allergic to school dances." Or "There's a cricket match I'd rather watch that night."

There were a gazillion reasons for Oliver to say no, and unfortunately I'd spent the last few days thinking up new ones.

"What happened?" I asked, leaning so far forward I almost fell off the bench.

"Yeah, don't keep us in suspense," said Rachel.

Claire huffed out another breath. "I asked him and he said yes."

"Wait, that's a bad thing?" Emma raised one eyebrow.

She wasn't the only confused one. All of my friends seemed completely bewildered. And this was good because it kept their attention away from me.

I was not simply perplexed. I felt majorly disappointed. Tears sprung to my eyes. I blinked fast to keep them from falling as I tried to come to terms with the news.

Oliver said yes. Well, of course he did. I'd tried to prepare myself for this situation. I'd even practiced my reaction to the news in the bathroom mirror the other day just in case I found myself in this exact situation.

Eyes wide, bright smile, both thumbs up. "That's awesome!" I planned on saying. But instead, my throat felt swollen and dry. So much so that I couldn't manage to say a word.

Which makes no sense because deep down, I should've known that Claire would ask Oliver, eventually. She liked him too much not to. Just like I knew Oliver was a nice guy who wouldn't say no unless he had a really good reason to.

I guess I just hoped something would happen before this moment arrived.

Like, he'd ask me.

Or Claire would change her mind.

Or the president would cancel Valentine's Day and all activities relating to the holiday for reasons of national security.

But now it was too late.

My chest ached, like someone had played Ping-Pong with my heart, which then rolled off the table and got stomped on.

"What's the problem?" asked Rachel.

I looked up, afraid she'd noticed my reaction, but all eyes were still on Claire.

"It's the way he said yes," she explained. "Like, totally unenthusiastically. This was my first time asking a boy to a dance, my first time asking a boy anything important, and I guess I just thought it would be bigger. More eventful. It's not like I was expecting fireworks or anything dumb like that. It's just, well, I guess I just wanted him to be as psyched as I was. Or even a little psyched."

"You mean he wasn't?" I asked, hopeful.

"Not really," Claire said.

"Maybe he just wanted to play it cool," said Emma.

"If that's the case, he deserves an Academy Award."

"Tell us what happened," said Emma. "Like, second by second."

Claire took a deep breath before explaining. "I waited until he was alone at his locker and I walked up to him and said, 'Hey, mind if I ask you something?' And he said, 'No.' And I said, 'No, I can't ask you?' And he said, 'No, as in no, I don't mind.' And then we both laughed. And then I said, 'I was thinking—wouldn't it be fun to go to the dance?' And he said, 'Yeah—I am going.' And I said, 'No, I mean together.' And then he sort of paused before saying, 'Okay, fine.'"

"Okay is good," said Emma.

"Okay is *okay* and just barely," Claire said. "But *fine*? *Fine* is not what anyone wants to hear, especially in his totally unenthusiastic tone. It sounded more like he was agreeing to let me borrow his pencil."

"But to be fair, Oliver is way into his pencils," Yumi joked.

"Not funny!" said Claire. "And I didn't tell you the worst part."

"There's something worse than *okay*?" asked Rachel.

"Don't forget about the pause," I said.

"See, you guys totally know how bad this is!" Claire exclaimed. "When he said, 'Okay, fine,' he shrugged."

Emma cringed.

"Yikes!" said Rachel.

Claire clutched her head with both hands and leaned her elbows on the table. "Shrugging is really bad, right? Everyone knows shrugging is bad. It's like he's telling me he doesn't care. Like, it doesn't even matter. Who shrugs and says sure? Someone whose message is, 'Sure I'll go with you because I have nothing better to do that night.'"

"Are you absolutely positive that he shrugged at you?" asked Yumi.

Claire shot Yumi a look of frustration. "You think I imagined a shrug?"

"Well, was it a big shrug or a little shrug?"

Claire pondered this for a few moments. "Medium size."

"One shoulder or two?" asked Rachel.

"Two."

"And did he sort of tilt his head to one side when he did it?" asked Emma.

Claire blinked back tears. "I don't remember! Does it matter?"

Emma bit her bottom lip. "No, I guess it doesn't."

"A shrug can mean lots of things," said Yumi. "Maybe he was trying to itch his ears with his shoulders."

Claire looked at Yumi in silence, like her suggestion didn't even warrant a comment.

"Sorry," said Yumi.

"It's fine," said Claire. "But let me ask you this—has Nathan ever shrugged at you?"

"Well, no. I don't think so, but it's possible that Nathan shrugs all the time when we're texting."

"Doubtful," said Claire.

"Well, maybe he's just not a shrugger."

"I never thought of Oliver as a shrugger," said Claire.

"Maybe it's new for him."

"Why would he suddenly take up shrugging?" asked Claire.

"Who knows why boys do anything?" asked Rachel.

"Why is Erik going out with Hannah when he could go out with me?"

I should've said something to defend Hannah but I was too busy thinking. Was Claire overreacting? Or was Oliver really not that into going to the dance with her? And if not, was he *not* interested in the dance? Or was he just *not* interested in being Claire's date?

I thought back to our talk on the lawn. Oliver *might* have been asking me if I wanted to go with him. But if that were true, why didn't he ask me again? Because he was shy? Or because he thought I wasn't interested? Maybe he just hadn't gotten around to it yet. . . .

What if Oliver really did say yes to Claire to be nice? What would've happened if I'd asked him to the dance? Would he have shrugged and said fine? Or would he have seemed happier?

And what's wrong with me for thinking this?

"You're forgetting the most important point," said Rachel. "He said yes, and that means you get to go to the dance with a really cute boy—and not only that but the boy you like—instead of being stuck with your second choice."

Emma nodded. "She's got a point there."

"So what are you going to wear?" asked Yumi.

"Major dilemma," said Claire, sitting up straighter. "I don't want to look like I'm trying too hard, but I do need to look my best. And I'd like to wear something unique, but not wacky. There's such a fine line."

Claire seemed excited, like she'd already gotten over Oliver's shrug, and for some reason this annoyed me.

"Are you going to make something?" asked Rachel.

"Or borrow your sister's clothes?" asked Emma.

"Is your hair too short to wear up?" Yumi wondered. "Because if you do wear it up, you should totally wear dangly earrings."

As my friends asked Claire a million and three questions, I stared at my peanut butter and grape jelly sandwich, my handprints visible in the bread where I'd squeezed it too tightly.

I took a small bite and tried to focus on chewing but my mind wandered to the upcoming dance. It was taking place in the auditorium, this I knew. I imagined they'd transform the entire room. It would be dark and romantic, with twinkling lights and soft music.

Claire would look beautiful—even more beautiful than usual, that is. I imagined her in a long, flowing white dress, her hair pulled up in a loose bun, with tendrils brushing her bare collarbone.

I don't actually know what tendrils are, but last summer my friend Sophia brought this steamy romance novel to camp and she read it aloud to our entire bunk after lights-out. Whenever the heroine in the story went to a ball, she swept her hair up into a loose bun, with tendrils brushing her bare collarbone. So I knew that whatever it was, it had something to do with being grown-up and romantic.

Oliver would be all dressed up, too. Maybe with tendrils but probably that's just a girl thing, not a dance thing. I pictured him in a nice pair of jeans with his T-shirt tucked in. They'd enter the room arm in arm and everyone would look their way. They'd be the most stunning couple there. Maybe they'd even sparkle. Not because of body glitter but because of some magical, sparkly properties that they and they alone possessed due to their total spectacularness.

Then I imagined Oliver scanning the room, not to admire the decor but because he was searching for someone.

As in, someone other than his date.

Meanwhile I'd be standing in the corner by myself, leaning against the wall, like the decorating committee had run out of tape and had hired me to hold up the giant cardboard cupid.

I'd look up suddenly and our eyes would meet. Oliver would smile and tilt his head and I'd smile back, coyly. (Another thing I read about in that romance novel.) I'd offer a fluttery fingertip wave and then he'd approach.

Claire would be confused at first and maybe even upset. But once she saw that the feelings we had for each other were true and strong and mutual, not to mention electric in their intensity, she'd relent, knowing that she and Oliver just weren't meant to be.

Oliver would approach and ask, "May I have this dance?"

And I'd say, "What about the cardboard cupid cutout?"

And he'd say, "Forget about the cardboard cupid cutout. Let it fall."

Then my favorite slow song would come on but not coincidentally—Oliver would've requested it.

I'd back away from the wall. Cupid would fall. And then we'd dance.

Meanwhile, Claire would meet the love of her life—a tall and handsome transfer student who'd just moved to town from somewhere really romantic. Like Paris or Rome or maybe both.

She'd forget about Oliver, move on. This part was essential because I wanted the best for Claire. I truly did! I just knew that what was best for Claire did not involve Oliver in any way. It couldn't! Not when he paused and shrugged, which I now realized was clear evidence that he liked someone else—probably me.

"So what do you think?"

Someone poked me in the shoulder.

"Hello? Earth to Annabelle?"

I looked up with a start. "Huh?"

"You okay?" Claire stared at me with genuine concern. And that's when the guilt crept in.

What could I say? "Oh, I'm fine. I was just busy fantasizing about stealing your date." I don't think so.

But I had to say something because now everyone else stared, too. "Sorry," I said. "Um, what?"

"We need your input," Claire explained. "My sister

offered to lend me her favorite skirt, but is that like wearing something used? She wore it to school once, so what if Oliver notices and thinks it's weird? Like, I only get hand-me-downs because my moms can't afford to get me new clothes, which is not true at all. They're just really into recycling."

"I don't think Oliver thinks that way. He doesn't have a mean bone in his body. And anyway, boys don't notice stuff like that."

Claire popped two grapes in her mouth, contemplating as she chewed. "So maybe I should spring for something new. I've been saving my allowance for a few months now."

Oh, who cares? That was my first thought—one so rude, I barely recognized myself. I knew I was being unfair. Mean, even, when all Claire had ever been was kind and generous and funny and sweet.

I was a lousy friend for having these thoughts.

No, I was a lousy person. And I needed to make it up to her. That's why I said, "Hey, want some help? I could come over one day after school and we can go through your closet."

Claire smiled. "That sounds fun!"

And that's how—a few days later—I found myself at Claire's house, helping her find an outfit so she could steal my crush.

# chapter fourteen
## the anti-fashion show

**N**ormally anything related to Claire and clothes is tons of fun. But when we got to her house after school on Thursday, all I felt was dread.

Claire—completely oblivious to my misery—opened up her closet and began pulling out clothes. Here's what ended up on the floor within the first thirty seconds:

> silver leggings
> purple miniskirt
> ballet flats with red rhinestones
> black puffy vest with a faux-fur collar.

At least I assumed it was faux fur, since I couldn't imagine Claire—or any of my friends—ever wearing the real thing.

"I found it," Claire yelled, putting on a blue wrap dress with a purple sash. "What do you think?" She turned around and did her best imitation of a runway model, kicking her clothes aside as she strutted across the room, with one hand on her hip.

"I like it," I said.

"Think it would look better with boots or ballet flats?"

Did it really matter? I wanted to ask her, but I stopped myself because of course it mattered. She was going to the dance with Oliver. Everything mattered. But if I said that I'd reveal too much so I simply replied, "Either way."

Claire sighed. "My favorite boots have heels but that would make me so much taller than him."

"You're already taller than him," I couldn't help but point out.

"Right. So why make myself more so? That's the problem with sixth grade boys!"

"They're not all short." I took a deep breath. "But if Oliver's height bothers you, then maybe you should go with someone else. Like what about Sanjay? He's tall. Cute, too."

Claire wrinkled her nose. "He's one of those guys who drums on his desk with his fingers."

"Because he plays the drums."

Claire shrugged. "Still annoying." She took off the dress and continued tearing through her closet.

I sat down on her bed right in time for her to throw a beaded jean jacket on me, without even noticing. I pulled it off my head. "Um, Claire?"

She spun around. "Oops, sorry!"

I held up the jacket. "This is cute. How come you never wear it?"

"I wore it all the time last year and I got sick of it. Want to take it?"

"Really?" I slipped into the jacket and admired myself in front of Claire's full-length mirror. The jacket was faded and perfectly broken in, with a hand-embroidered row of ladybugs marching out of one pocket.

"Not to keep, but you can borrow it for a while."

"Thanks. It's perfect. I'll wear it tomorrow and Oliver is going to love it."

Claire looked up suddenly. "What?"

"Nothing!" I said. "It's just fitting, since our science fair project involves bugs and last week the gardener released a whole slew of ladybugs in his backyard in order to save the rosebushes from aphids. Apparently ladybugs eat them. So we were overrun. It was hilarious and we considered focusing on just ladybugs but—"

Claire interrupted me. "Oliver has rosebushes? Maybe I should ask him to make me a corsage for the dance."

I shook my head. "Rachel said corsages are a high school thing."

"Oh." Claire twisted up her hair and then let it fall. "Hey, think I should wear skinny jeans with boots and a sparkly top?" she asked, trying on that exact outfit.

"Looks great," I said.

She walked over to the mirror and turned from left to right. Then she checked herself out from behind. Annoyingly, she looked amazing from every angle.

"Did you know that Oliver's mom used to model in Europe?" said Claire. "That's how she met his dad."

I didn't know this. And it bothered me that Claire did.

"He ran an advertising company and she was the face of one of his campaigns," she went on, like she was some Oliver expert. "They met at a party in Italy and fell in love."

"How do you even know that?" I asked.

"My mom told me. She and Oliver's mom do yoga together and sometimes they go out for coffee after."

I wished my mom did yoga. Then maybe she'd be friends with Oliver's mom, too.

Claire paused and looked at me thoughtfully. Eyes narrowed slightly, staring like she saw through me to the core of my inner lousy-friend being.

I was about to open my mouth to confess and apologize when she said, "Know what would look really cute with that jacket? My striped boatneck shirt."

She strode across the room to her overflowing dresser and opened up the bottom drawer. "I could've sworn it was here somewhere. Ha! I almost forgot about this." Instead of the shirt, she held up a yellow and red striped, sequined miniskirt. "Olivia took me vintage clothes shopping for my birthday last year, and we both decided to buy the craziest, most out-rageous outfits we could find, and then we wore them to the mall and split up and kept track of how many weird looks we got."

"Who won?" I asked.

"We kind of tied." Claire tossed me the skirt and said, "Try it on."

I held it up with two fingers. "This thing looks like a disco ball vomited on a Hot-Dog-on-a-Stick uniform."

"And you say that like it's a bad thing!" said Claire.

I shrugged and slipped the skirt on over my leggings.

Then Claire handed me an orange stretchy top.

"I think this clashes," I said.

"That's the point." Claire wrapped herself in a flow-ery ruffled apron. Then she stepped into a pair of kelly green platform heels. "I'm sick of looking for something perfect to wear. Let's focus on being anti-fashion for a while. And we need music, too." She hurried over to her Mac and selected one of her famous '80s playlists.

As Madonna blasted from the computer, Claire handed me a purple feathered boa and wrapped a pink one around her own neck.

Then we both strutted around the room like we were models on a catwalk or something.

When I tripped over one of Claire's stray boots she laughed, which gave me the giggles.

Then we tried on some more outrageous outfits until Claire decided something was missing. "Makeup!" she declared out of nowhere, sitting down at her sis-ter's dressing table and opening the top drawer. It was filled with lipsticks and eye shadows and mascaras, plus mysterious tubs and brushes of all sizes. Also, a metal device that looked like it could be used for torture. "What's this?" I asked, holding it up.

"Eyelash curler. Want to try it?"

"Nope." I put it away quickly. "You're sure Olivia won't mind us using her stuff?"

Claire puckered her lips at her mirror image and applied some bright purple lipstick. Then she spun around, grinned, and batted her eyelashes. "Olivia won't mind at all. Especially since she'll never know. She's at softball practice for another hour. Come on. Your turn."

She sat me down in the little chair and brushed on some purple eye shadow.

"Isn't that kind of thick?" I asked.

"It only feels that way because you never wear makeup." She put it away and grabbed some blush, eyeliner, and lipstick. And five minutes later, she turned me around so I could see myself in the mirror. "Voilà!"

I blinked at myself. "I look like a clown."

Claire tilted her head at our reflections. "Know what we need?"

"A washcloth?" I guessed.

"Sparkle!" She added some body glitter to her cheeks and then mine. Then she pulled out her digital camera and snapped some shots. I posed with my hip jutted out, my lower lip thrust, and my arms crossed.

"Work it!" said Claire.

Two minutes later I asked to see the shots. Claire passed over the camera and said, "You look amazing!"

Flipping through the images, I shook my head. "This is so not me!"

"It is you, and you look fabulous!"

"Your turn!" I aimed the camera at Claire.

She vamped it up for a while and then we turned on the self-timer, balancing the camera on the book-shelf so we could get some glam shots together.

We were having so much fun that I completely forgot I was helping Claire get ready for a date with my secret crush. At least until the phone rang.

"Claire!" her mom yelled from downstairs. "It's for you."

Claire turned off the music and rushed to the phone. "Hello? Oh, hey Rach. What's up?"

I went back to the mirror and made funny faces at myself, not eavesdropping, exactly, but since we were in the same room I couldn't help but overhear her end of the conversation.

"He said yes? That's awesome! So we're all set. Great. I can't wait. Omigosh, I have nothing to wear!" She glanced at the pile of clothes on her floor, then turned to me and smiled. "Annabelle will help. Yeah. Great. Okay, see you."

"Help with what?" I asked after she hung up.

"Help me figure out what to wear on my first date."

Of course. How could I forget? "I thought we were already doing that."

"That's for the dance. I'm talking about Satur-day night. Oliver and I are going bowling with Rachel and Caleb."

"Oh, cool," I replied, thinking this news was anything but. I just hoped my "surprised and horrified" expression would be mistaken for an "I'm so excited for you" face.

But Claire didn't even glance my way as she fixed her bangs in the mirror. "I've never had this much trouble figuring out what to wear."

I sank down to the edge of her bed, hardly believing that Claire was going bowling with Oliver.

I took another tissue and tried to wipe off the glitter, but instead it spread. "I can't get this stupid stuff off!"

"What's wrong?" asked Claire, finally noticing I was still there.

I swallowed the lump in my throat and coughed. "Nothing. Bowling sounds casual so you need to wear jeans."

"How about a vintage bowling shirt?" she asked. "Or would that look like I was trying too hard?"

"Trying too hard to do what?"

"Okay, good point. Now the problem is, my baggy jeans look better with the vintage shirt but my skinny jeans are way more flattering. But if I wear them on Saturday I can't wear them again to the dance unless we have at least two dates in between outfits and there's hardly enough time for—"

Suddenly Claire turned to me and smiled. "Hey you should come," she said.

"Really?" For a quick second I thought that I was overreacting. Maybe I misheard Claire and she and

Oliver weren't planning a date. Maybe it was just, like, an outing. Something all my friends could go to—as a big group. Totally innocent. It made sense. I mean, bowling? What's romantic about bowling? Nothing. In that romance novel, no one went bowling, ever. "I guess I could probably make it," I said.

"Perfect! So, who are you going to ask?"

"Ask?"

"Yeah—as your date. I mean if it weren't just me and Oliver and Rachel and Caleb, it wouldn't be a big deal. But I don't want you to feel like the fifth wheel. You should find someone, anyway. You know, for the dance."

"Right!" I swallowed hard. "Of course I'd need to find a date." I took another tissue from the box and pretended to wipe off the eye shadow. Except really I just needed an excuse to hide my eyes, which were tearing up like crazy.

"You okay?" asked Claire. "It almost looks like you're—"

"I'm not crying." I shook my head and sniffed. "I think I'm just allergic. You know, to all the makeup."

"Oh no! Let me get my mom's cold cream. I'll be right back."

Claire rushed from the room, returning moments later with a blue bottle and some cotton balls. "Even better—I found actual eye-makeup remover and it's for sensitive skin."

After she helped me clean my face, my skin felt raw and tingly and my eyes were still glassy.

I blinked hard, stood up, and grabbed my back-pack. "I should go. I'm not feeling so great."

"Don't forget the jacket," Claire said in a sing-songy chipper voice. "And feel better!"

I'm glad Claire bought my excuse. Not that I was making anything up, exactly.

It's true—I did feel completely lousy.

Just not physically so.

## chapter fifteen
### hannah's nonnews

As soon as I got to science the next day Tobias said, "I typed up all our field notes, and I've also been doing extra reading and guess what? It turns out a ladybug isn't a bug at all. It's a beetle."

"Really?" I asked.

Tobias nodded. "Yup. And technically, it's called a *Coccinella septempuntata*."

"A what?"

Tobias repeated himself, enunciating carefully like he'd been up practicing all night. "Co-cin-el-la sep-tem-punta-ta."

It impressed me how into the project Tobias was. If I overlooked all of his teasing, I'd have to admit I was glad he was on our team. And yes, his face got pretty pimply sometimes, but his hair flopped over his eyes in a way that almost looked cute.

I wondered if he liked bowling.

Maybe I should ask him. Then I wouldn't have to sit home alone on Saturday night, stressing over what might be happening at the Bowl-A-Rama. I'd get to

see it all firsthand. Although maybe it would be torture, watching Claire and Oliver on a date together.
What if they flirted? Or worse. What if they held hands
or kissed or something? That wasn't something I could
bear to witness.

Unless imagining all that stuff was worse than
actually watching it happen.

I couldn't decide. But then I had another thought.
Maybe it wasn't so nice, using Tobias like that.

Only asking him so I could go out and spy on my
best friend and my crush.

Unless I told him ahead of time that we'd only be
going as friends.

Or would that sound too dorky considering how
obvious it was that we'd never be more than just
friends? Especially when, at the moment, he smelled
like modeling clay?

Before I could decide whether or not to ask him,
he opened his mouth and let out a hugely loud burp.

"Awesome," said Jonathan, who sits at the table
behind us.

Tobias grinned and burped again.

"You're the master!" Jonathan stuck out his hand,
and when Tobias gave him a high five, he burped for
a third time.

Ugh! Clearly asking Tobias out on a date would be
worse than staying home alone.

I spent the rest of the day trying to find a boy I
wouldn't mind going on a triple date with, but no one

seemed as good as Oliver. Who, by the way, was wearing a new green T-shirt that really brought out the color in his eyes.

So I gave up searching and made plans to hit the mall with Yumi and Emma instead.

When Saturday night rolled around we found ourselves in line at the multiplex on the top floor.

"Hey, how come you're not bowling with everyone else tonight?" I asked Emma.

"Same reason as you. No date."

"But you have a boyfriend who lives here," said Yumi. "If Nathan lived closer, I'm sure we'd be bowling right now—no offense."

"None taken," said Emma, twisting her mouth up unhappily. "I asked Phil but he said no because he needs to work on his science fair project all weekend."

"How long does it take to build a hamster maze?" I asked.

"Oh, he finished the maze-building part last week. Now he's making Einstein run it ten times a night."

"He can't take a break on a Saturday night?" asked Yumi.

Emma shook her head. "Einstein's training schedule is very strict."

"Poor hamster," I said.

Emma shrugged. "I understand it. He just really wants to win."

"Me, too."

"I would if it weren't for Hawaii," Yumi said.

"You mean if it weren't for Nathan," I said.

Yumi grinned. "Nathan and Hawaii. Same difference. I won't deny it."

"Who's gonna take care of Einstein if Phil gets to go to Space Camp?" I wondered.

"He'd probably try to sneak him in," Emma said. "Phil is crazy about that hamster!"

"Does that mean he's taking him to the dance?" Yumi asked as we both laughed.

"I hope not," said Emma. "Hey, have you guys figured out what to wear?"

"Last night I tried on six outfits," I admitted. "But then I felt silly because I don't even have a date. So it's not like it matters."

"Don't feel bad. It's not like I have one, either," said Yumi.

"Wait—didn't we decide that you're going with Dante?" asked Emma.

"You guys decided," said Yumi. "But it's up to me and I don't want to do that to him."

Not having a date by choice was very different from not having a date because your best friend stole him. But at least I wouldn't be the only one of my friends going solo.

When we got to the front of the line we bought our tickets and went inside. The movie was good but not good enough to distract me from thinking about Oliver's big date with Claire.

Were they bowling right now? How did they split

up for teams? Girls versus boys? Or couple versus couple? Who was keeping score? Did Claire go with skinny jeans or baggy? Did they order nachos or hot dogs or both?

Claire told me she stunk at bowling and worried she'd get five gutter balls in a row, which would obviously be humiliating, but I knew Oliver was too nice to make fun of her. But would she really get five in a row? And if so, wouldn't he think that was pretty bad? And, like, maybe wish he were bowling with someone else? Someone with more experience whose grandma lives near one of the biggest bowling alleys in the whole city?

I'm just saying . . .

After the movie we headed up to the food court for pizza, but before we got there we saw Hannah in the window of a fancy dress shop. The kind where you can get silk shoes custom-dyed to match any outfit.

When she saw me waving she motioned for us to come in the store, so we went. Musak played softly. Two women strolled by with fancy little dogs in their purses.

"What's up?" I asked, stopping short once I noticed Taylor was there as well.

Taylor looked us up and down in her judgey way—not exactly hostile, just very Taylor-esque.

"We're looking for dresses for the dance," Hannah said, tucking her hair behind her ears.

Taylor held up a purple slinky, strapless thing.

"Wouldn't this look amazingly fab on Hannah? She's got just the right bone structure to pull it off."

I'd no idea what that meant but said, "Yeah, I guess," because I didn't want to fight. If I were honest I'd tell her that the dress looked like something an evil princess would wear. Plus, Hannah and I had already agreed that strapless dresses were too annoying to deal with.

"See, I told you it's gorgeous. Try it on." Taylor shoved the dress at her.

Hannah took a small step away from it. "That's okay. I don't have enough money on me, anyway."

Taylor rolled her eyes. "Just try it, dummy. If you love it, they'll put it on hold for you and your mom can buy it tomorrow."

"I'm at my dad's this weekend, and I don't think he'll want to go dress shopping. He gets all squirmy whenever I ask him to do stuff like that. He'd probably get my stepmom to take me, and I just know she'd try to talk me into getting something pink or something from the half-off rack. Or something that's pink and half off."

"Fine. Whatever." Taylor let out an annoyed huff of breath and put the dress back on the rack. "You're just upset about Erik."

"Are you guys fighting?" asked Emma.

"No," said Hannah. "Everything is great."

"Except he still hasn't asked her to the dance," said Taylor.

"He still hasn't?" asked Yumi.

"What do you mean 'still'?" said Hannah. "The dance is two weeks away. He's got plenty of time."

As Hannah and Taylor went back to dress shopping, Yumi, Emma, and I all looked at each other. No one said anything, but we didn't have to. Obviously, we were all thinking the same thing: something was up.

## chapter sixteen
### no candy, no balloons, no nuts, and no carrots

So then they were all, 'I can't believe she bowled another gutter ball,'" Rachel said at lunch on Tuesday.

Of the four of us, only Claire laughed. Rachel didn't notice and kept talking. "And Claire was like, 'Excuse me for not being an expert bowler. But who wants to be great at bowling? People who like wearing used shoes?' And—"

"And Oliver was taking a sip of root beer when she said it, and he cracked up and sprayed soda everywhere," Claire finished, smiling triumphantly.

"It would've been gross if it wasn't so funny," Rachel added as the two of them giggled.

Yumi ignored them because she was texting Nathan under the table.

And Emma just looked away, her mouth set in a straight line and a bored expression on her face, like she was sick of this story.

I didn't blame her. It's the third time they'd told us about how Oliver sprayed root beer out of his mouth. We were tired of hearing about their fabulous double date.

"Know what's so weird about Caleb?" asked Rachel. "And I mean weird in a good way."

"How he acts like a clueless surfer dude, but he's really into animals and he even volunteers to clean out the rabbit cages at the local shelter, which is the grossest job there is," said Emma.

"How did you know?" asked Rachel.

"Because you told us yesterday," Emma replied.

"Oh." Rachel took a bite of her tuna fish sandwich. "Sorry."

"Hey, I heard the no-Candygrams go on sale next week," said Claire.

"What's a no-Candygram?" I asked.

"Well, you know what a regular Candygram is, right?" asked Claire.

After I shook my head, she went on to explain. "It's when you pay a dollar and you get to write a message on a card that will be delivered with some candy to the person of your choice on Valentine's Day."

"They hand them out in homeroom," Rachel added.

"And the no-Candygram is just the card?" I guessed.

Emma nodded. "Exactly. They took away our candy after some parents complained that childhood obesity is on the rise. They wanted to send balloons instead. But then the environmentalists asked, 'Why bring more nonrecyclable waste into the area?' So someone thought trail mix would be better, but then the parents of kids with nut allergies got together and protested. Which is how everyone came to agree on carrot sticks, but that seemed like way too much work. So now we're just doing grams."

"No candy, no carrots, no nothing," said Yumi.

"Except for the cards and message, which is the best part anyway," Rachel said.

"Huh. Guess I don't need to worry about any of that, since I don't have a date for the dance." I didn't mean to sound all sour cherries about it. It just came out that way.

"They're not just for dates. You're supposed to get them for all your best friends, too," Claire said.

"Are you sending one to Caleb?" Yumi asked Rachel.

"I probably should," said Rachel. "Since he's so nice to rabbits and all, but I don't want him to get the wrong idea."

"What's the wrong idea?" I asked.

"That's the problem." Rachel frowned. "I mean, I kind of like him and I'm sure we'll have fun at the dance, but it'll also be weird seeing Erik there with Hannah."

"If they end up going," Yumi said.

Rachel perked up. "What do you mean 'if'?"

"Nothing," said Yumi. "Just—we ran into Hannah at the mall on Saturday, and we found out he hasn't asked her yet."

"As of Saturday or as of today?" Rachel wondered.

No one answered her, so she looked at me. "Anna-belle? What do you know? This is important!"

"She told us on Saturday and I haven't heard anything since, but we don't really talk about it, so maybe he's asked her by now."

Rachel munched on her celery stick in contemplation. "Maybe I should send him a gram."

"Erik?" I asked.

She nodded. "Of course, Erik."

"That's bold," said Claire.

"If you do send him one, you've got to get one for Caleb, too. He's your date, so it's only fair," said Emma.

"Anyway, just sending one isn't the main issue," said Claire. "It's all about what you write in the note."

"Dear Erik," said Rachel, pretending to write in the air with her celery stick. "Why go out with Hannah when you can have me instead?"

Everyone giggled. Sure it was a tad mean-spirited, but it was funny, too.

"And Dear Caleb," Rachel continued. "You're a great second choice. Thanks for being my backup date."

"What if I send one to Oliver and he doesn't send one to me?" Claire said.

"He will," said Rachel. "Oliver is way too polite not to."

"I don't want him to send me one because he's polite," said Claire. "I want him to send me one because he likes me."

"Obviously he likes you," I said. "You guys had the best time bowling."

"I mean, I want him to *like* me like me," said Claire. "But half the time he talked about stupid stuff, like cricket or your science fair project."

"He mentioned our project?" I asked.

"Uh-huh." Claire nodded.

I leaned a little closer. "What did he say?"

"He talked about how much fun it was, learning about bugs and stuff. And that if you weren't on the team, he and Tobias would never get anything done. And I was like, 'Please can we not talk about school on Saturday night?'"

"You should see the bug drawings he's doing. They're incredible. He's so talented."

Claire gave me this look—like she could read my mind and wasn't exactly thrilled with what she found there. So I quickly asked her, "How's your project coming along?"

"Fine." Claire shrugged. "We're almost done."

I turned to Emma and Rachel. "What about you guys?"

"It's crazy," said Rachel. "You wouldn't believe the high fat and sugar content in the food here. It's all so processed and prepackaged. The only real actual fruit they sell are apples, and half the time they're mushy."

"Or at least they have mushy spots," Emma added. "But Phil doesn't think we can win because my project is anti-school."

"How is it anti-school?" I asked. "It's science. You're just reporting the facts."

"Right." Emma nodded.

"I think he's just trying to psych you out," said Rachel.

"But why would he do that?" asked Emma. "He's my boyfriend."

It was a good question, but not one that any of us could answer.

## chapter seventeen
to no-candygram or not to no-candygram?
that is the question . . .

Today is the last day to buy no-Candy grams," Rachel informed me on our walk to school a couple of days later. "So I'm taking a vote. Should I send one to Erik or not?"

"I say no," I replied. "Which is what I already told you three, no, four times."

"What about you?" Rachel asked Yumi.

"Huh?" Yumi looked up from her phone.

"It's dangerous to text while walking," Rachel said. "You could trip and hurt yourself. Or you could hurt your best friend's feelings by not paying attention to what she's saying."

"Sorry." Yumi flashed a sheepish smile and then put her phone away.

"So?" asked Rachel. "Erik—should I send him a gram or not?"

"I thought we covered this ages ago. If you send one to Erik, you've gotta send one to Caleb, too. Otherwise, it's mean."

"But that's two whole dollars."

"It's all or nothing," said Yumi.

Rachel threw up her hands. "You guys are no help! You'll be lucky if you get any no-Candygrams from me."

"You mean you haven't already sent them?" asked Yumi.

"No, I'm just kidding. Of course I have."

"Me too," said Yumi.

I stayed silent because I'd been avoiding the no-Candygram table all week. The problem? Besides wanting to send them to Rachel, Emma, Yumi, and Claire, I really wanted to get one for Oliver, too.

We were lab partners, after all. And he totally deserved one, since he was always sneaking ginger cookies into class for me. We were friends, just like me and Claire and Emma and Yumi and Rachel. So I don't know why I hesitated.

But I did. And it's not like I could ask for any advice. That would make things way too obvious.

As soon as we got to school I checked my wallet for the five dollars my mom gave me. It was still there, so I headed over to the no-Candygram table.

A bored-looking eighth grader sat behind the booth. It had a red tablecloth and some balloons on either side, and I wondered what the environmentalists thought of that. Maybe not much, since it was only a handful.

By the time I got to the front of the line I still hadn't decided, so I asked for four grams and handed her my money.

"Here you go," she said, handing me the cards along with my change. I stared at the single dollar, thinking I should've just bought five and then decided later. Now I'd have to wait in line all over again. If I were to get one for Oliver, that is.

"Hello?" She waved the money at me impatiently.

"Sorry, I'll take another one. Unless. Well, no. Never mind." I grabbed the dollar and shoved it into my back pocket.

Then I wrote messages to my friends.

*To Emma, aka "Ms. Smarty-Brain" (I'd say pants, but I know you have a problem with that): According to the U.S. Greeting Card Association, over 1 billion Valentine's Day cards are sent out every year. And I guess that makes this 1 billion and 1. (Okay, it only took a Wikipedia search to come up with that statistic, and I know how you feel about online source material, but too bad!)*
    *☺♥★Annabelle*

*To Rachel: So glad we get to walk to school together every day and that we're always so early! Happy Valentine's Day! You were my first real friend in Westlake. That is cool.*
    *☺♥★Annabelle*

*To Yumi: This is not as good as a card from your darling Nathan, but since he doesn't go to school here, you'll have to settle for second best! Here's to a winning season for my favorite pitcher! And if you do go to*

*Hawaii this summer, do you think I might fit in your suitcase?*

☺♥★*Annabelle*

*To Claire: Happy Valentine's Day to my most fashion-forward friend. Thanks for being so stylish.*

☺♥★*Annabelle*

After signing the last card, I went back to the table. "Is today really the last day?" I asked as I handed her the notes.

The eighth grader nodded. "Yup."

"Does that mean you're here after school, too? Or just through lunch?"

"Look," she said impatiently, "if you want to send another gram, you should do it now because we're almost out." She pointed to a small stack of blank cards.

"That's all that's left?" I asked.

"Yup."

I stared at the pile. This was my last chance. Do I send one to Oliver or would that be wrong? No. Yes. No. No. Yes. No. Wait a minute. Does no mean it wouldn't be wrong so it would actually be okay? Or does no mean no gram? Of course, since they're no-Candygrams maybe the double negative cancels out my negative answer, which means that yes, I should definitely buy him one.

I pulled the dollar out of my pocket and slammed it down on the counter. "I need one more, please."

"Here you go." The girl pushed a blank card my way.

I clicked open my pen and hovered over the card, wanting to change my mind but knowing it was too late. The eighth grader was staring and I'd already acted too wishy-washy. This was getting embarrassing!

But what was I supposed to write? I mean, besides the obvious *Dear Oliver*.

Since the grams were being delivered on February 14, I quickly scrawled *Happy Valentine's Day!*

But then I couldn't think of anything else to say so I just signed the note *Sincerely, Annabelle Stevens.*

As soon as I finished I realized my message sounded kind of dumb, not to mention generic and boring. And why did I use my last name? There's no other Annabelle in school. Not one who spells her name like me, anyway, and not one who is friends with Oliver, as far as I know.

I couldn't write, *Hey, Oliver. I've got a massive crush on you so how about you ditch Claire, one of my very best friends, who's extra kind to animals and people, too, and beautiful (but lousy at bowling), and go to the dance with me instead? Love (in a friendly, not-totally-obsessed-with-you way because I'm only a smidgen obsessed), Annabelle.*

No, that might scare him. It scared *me* a little.

Yet the message I did write was so boring, I got sleepy just rereading it. No way could I send it. I turned back to the eighth grader. "Um, I messed up. Think I can have another?"

"Sure. For another dollar," she replied.

"But I don't have any more money," I cried.

"Okay, fine. Here you go." She pushed over another blank card and I crumpled the one I'd already written. Then I uncrumpled it and tore it into a bunch of little pieces instead. And shoved them into the bottom of my backpack because it seemed safer to dispose of them at home. If lighting matches didn't make me nervous I'd burn them, but maybe that was too extreme, anyway.

I stood there trying to come up with a better message and wishing I'd written something ahead of time, but I hadn't. And nothing new came to me, so I just wrote the same boring thing all over again, minus my last name.

As I handed it over, I glanced around just to make sure none of my friends were nearby. And that's when I got this funny feeling in my stomach. Not quite regret—just a twinge of strangeness, like I was being sneaky.

I didn't want anyone to know I'd sent Oliver a gram, and it felt weird keeping it a secret. But I justified it to myself. No one said I had to share my every move with my friends. True, they'd been talking about the no-Candygrams all week, and I knew exactly who was sending grams to whom, but I certainly wasn't required to share this information.

Anyway, it's not like I kept it from them on purpose. No one asked if I was sending a no-Candygram to Oliver. If they had, I'd have fessed up. Probably.

Well, maybe.

Okay, no, but that didn't matter because no one asked and no one ever would. My friends would never find out, and even if they did, there's nothing wrong with sending Oliver a no-Candygram.

Which is why I didn't understand the weird feeling I had in the pit of my stomach. Because it felt like I was doing something wrong. Something very, very wrong . . .

Once I handed over the gram, I spun around to leave and ran right into Hannah. Literally.

"Are you okay?" I bent down to help her pick up the books I'd knocked out of her arms.

"Fine," she sniffed. "Great." She marched past me to the no-Candygram table and asked, "Is it too late to get one of my grams back?"

"We don't offer refunds," the girl replied.

"I don't need my money back. All I need is the gram."

The eighth grader rolled her eyes and said, "You sixth graders and all your drama! Who's the card to?"

Hannah sniffed again. "Erik Wilson," she said.

The eighth grader began riffling through her box of already-filled-in grams.

Meanwhile, I hung around—partly out of curiosity but mostly to make sure Hannah was all right.

After she got back her gram—and tore it up—I asked, "Are you okay?"

"Fine," she sniffed. "Great now."

"Um, was that gram for Erik your boyfriend?" I asked.

"Nope," said Hannah. "It was for Erik my ex."

## chapter eighteen
### snickers packs a punch

I didn't know whether or not to tell Rachel about Hannah's news because I didn't want to seem gossipy, and I knew it was wrong to talk about people behind their backs, but luckily (for me, anyway) the information spread fast. The big Hannah-and-Erik breakup was all anyone could talk about at lunch the next day. And strangely no one seemed more upset than Rachel.

"Wait, isn't this good news?" I asked.

"It's great news that they broke up," said Rachel. "And rotten news that I already have a date for the dance."

"But last week you said Caleb was cute," said Claire. "And that you might be interested."

"*Maybe* is what I said," Rachel clarified. "But now that Erik is single I know for sure. I'd much rather go with him. You guys don't think I could cancel on Caleb?"

"No way," Yumi said, looking up from her phone. "The dance is this Saturday. You can't ditch him for someone else. That would be cruel."

"And anyway, what if Erik says no?" asked Claire.

"Good point," said Rachel. "I'd have to ask him before I dumped Caleb."

"That's wrong," I told her. "Caleb's a good guy. You said so yourself."

"I know, I know," said Rachel. "Caleb would be perfect if it weren't for Erik. But you can't help who you like."

Tell me about it!

I didn't realize I was staring at Claire until she turned to me and asked, "Is everything okay, Annabelle? Because you're acting weird, again."

"Again?" I asked.

And before Claire had a chance to tell me what she was talking about, Emma hurried over and sat down next to me. "Sorry I'm late," she said, "but you'll never guess what happened."

"Erik and Hannah?" asked Rachel. "We already know."

"No, I'm talking about Phil. His hamster died!"

"Oh no!" said Rachel.

"That's terrible!" cried Yumi. "What happened?"

Emma blinked back tears as she explained. "Einstein broke into his food supply—you know, all the junk food that Phil had been feeding him for his science experiment. And he ate it all and it was just too much for his tiny tummy. So basically, he gorged himself to death."

"Wait, you mean his stomach exploded?" I asked.

"Yes," Emma cried. "And I feel so bad. I mean, it's sad enough to lose your favorite pet, but poor Phil feels like it's all his fault, and now he doesn't even have a science project and he doesn't know what to do."

"Bummer," said Rachel.

"Unless we let him join our team," Emma added quickly.

"Wait, what?" Rachel put down her sandwich. "We can't be partners with Phil. Not after you asked him to work with you ages ago and he said no. It's not fair. We've already worked so hard! And we're almost done."

Emma bit her bottom lip.

"Tell me you didn't offer," said Rachel.

"I didn't have to because he asked," said Emma.

"Tell me you didn't say yes."

"Of course not," said Emma. "The science fair is only three days away and we're mostly done. But when I explained that to him, he accused me of being a lousy girlfriend. And also? He said that as a future great scientist of America, I should learn how to cooperate better with other people."

"He seemed to think differently a few weeks ago," said Rachel. "When he was so excited about beating us."

"That's exactly what I told him, but it didn't go over so well. He thinks I'm too competitive."

"He's the competitive one," said Rachel.

"Are you guys still together?" asked Yumi.

"And are you still going to the dance?" Claire asked.

"Yes and yes," Emma replied, although she didn't sound excited about either prospect.

She unpacked her lunch and lined it up in front of her—apple juice, peanut butter crackers, turkey avocado wrap, and vanilla wafer cookies all in a row. "I told Phil he should enter anyway. He's got Einstein on video and he could still bring in the maze. Even without the live demonstration it's still very impressive. And everyone knows you're supposed to show your entire methodology—even big mistakes. That's what real scientists do. But Phil is convinced that he's not going to win first prize with a failed experiment, so he's going to start from scratch."

"Poor Einstein," I said.

"Death by Snickers." Rachel shuddered.

"If it weren't so sad it would almost be funny," Yumi said.

"Almost," Emma replied, "but not quite."

## chapter nineteen
### check out the competition

**T**wo days later Oliver, Tobias, and I put the final touches on our Backyard Bugs project. We'd discovered that certain bugs, like ants and roly-polies, don't seem to care about colors, while others, like bumblebees and ladybugs, prefer blue. However, once we added sugar water to the mix, everything went out the window. Sugar water attracted bugs from everywhere, regardless of the color paper we used or even if we used paper at all. This we figured out after Tobias tripped and spilled a whole glass of our solution in the grass in between the yellow and blue pages. Everything swarmed.

He wanted to pretend it never happened, but I felt like it was important to include the mistake. And since it was my job to write out all of our conclusions, I won.

By the time we finished putting everything together, our project was way too big and bulky to transport on foot, so my mom gave us a ride back to school on Thursday evening.

"Do you want me to come in with you?" she asked as she pulled into the parking lot.

I'd already made her promise not to embarrass me on the ride over, so really it was the first thing she'd said besides, "Hello, Oliver and Tobias—it's very nice to meet you both." (Just like we'd practiced.)

"Just wait for us here," I said, adding, "please."

She smiled at me. "No problem. Good luck."

"Thanks, Mrs. Stevens," Oliver and Tobias both said as they scooted out of the car.

Luckily, we got a great table in the front corner of the room. Once we finished setting everything up, we stood back and admired our work. And I know it seems braggy to admit this, but I'm going to do it anyway. Our display was awesome.

All of our steps were written out, neatly, and the lines on our color-coded graph were perfectly straight. But what really made our project amazing were Oliver's drawings—complete with each bugs' proper scientific name. And as a bonus, we'd listed a bunch of random bug facts, too.

Here are some of my favorites:

Insects have been on this earth for 300 million years.

Lightning bugs and fireflies are actually beetles.

Ants can lift fifty times their weight.

After being decapitated, a cockroach head might stay alive for up to twelve hours.

Actually, Tobias made us include that last one, but we refused to let him test out the theory.

"This rocks," said Oliver.

"Duh!" Tobias replied.

"Let's check out the competition," I said, heading to the table next to us.

Monique and Lani had created their own paper out of recycled pizza boxes. They'd also figured out that if Birchwood Middle School canceled its required reading program, they could save five trees a year. It was an interesting idea, but their paper looked pretty lumpy and it also had grease stains. Plus, they only used two poster boards to describe their project (we'd used five). They didn't have any bonus material, either. Not to be overly critical.

The next three projects we passed were also on recycling.

"I told you all that environmental stuff was way too trendy," Tobias whispered as we stood in front of a pile of tin cans that had been turned into a sculpture of the Eiffel Tower.

Oliver leaned in close and whispered, "Is that even science?"

Neither Tobias nor I had an answer, and I doubted the judges would, either.

So far so good! On the other side of the gym, Emma and Rachel proved that half the food in our cafeteria is as fattening and as void of nutrients as a typical Happy Meal from McDonald's. Go Birchwood! Their whole project looked so impressive, I got nervous. But then I realized that if I couldn't win, I certainly wanted my friends to.

"Are you sure this is all true?" asked Tobias, pointing to their calorie graph.

"Positive," said Emma. "I quadruple-checked every single calculation."

"But how can a salad have the same amount of calories as a hamburger?" he asked.

"Cheese and bacon bits and ranch dressing," Rachel replied.

"Yum!" said Tobias as we moved onto the next project.

Jonathan had built an electric car with a remote control.

Jesse and Taylor made a clock out of a potato, which they'd decked out with pink Barbie heels and a little blond wig. I'm not sure why.

When we passed the fourth model volcano, Oliver punched Tobias in the arm and said, "Told you that was a dumb idea."

"There are some great projects here," I said. "But I think we still have a—"

Before I had a chance to say "chance," I saw the craziest, most elaborate and impressive science fair project in the entire gym. *Night Vision in Birds of Prey* read the fancy calligraphy sign. And it had everything— charts and graphs and complicated-looking equations and illustrations, plus five scary-looking birds, all carved out of soapstone and hand painted with such meticulous detail, they looked ready to take flight. Oh, and special glasses that allowed you to see like an eagle.

"I think you spoke too soon," Tobias whispered.

Oliver stared at the hawk and shivered. "That thing totally creeps me out."

I hopped to the right and left of the bird. "Its eyes follow you wherever you move."

"Intense," said Oliver.

The entire project seemed not just perfect but perfectly brilliant.

"Whoever did this is gonna win," said Tobias.

"I'll be sure to send you a postcard from Space Camp," someone said from behind us. "Or not."

I turned around to find myself face-to-face with Emma's boyfriend, Phil.

"This is yours?" I asked.

Phil nodded. "Yup."

"It's awesome," said Tobias, giving him a high five.

"Thanks," said Phil. "It took forever, carving and painting all those statues."

"You used oil paints, right?" asked Oliver. "Never mind, dumb question." He moved closer to the birds. "It's obviously oil work, but I can't tell if you used brushes or paint markers."

Phil hesitated.

"So which is it?" Oliver asked.

"Oh. Um, I don't remember," Phil answered.

Oliver looked at him like he was crazy. "What do you mean, you don't remember?"

"Kidding," said Phil—although none of us (including him) laughed. "Markers."

"Whenever I use paint markers, I can't get that kind of tiny detail just right—but this looks amazing," said Oliver. "What kind are they?"

"My mom bought them. So, uh, I don't really know," Phil told us. "Any more questions, or are you done giving me the third degree?"

"Sorry, dude!" Oliver backed away with his hands up. "Didn't mean to grill you. Best of luck. We'd better get going. Annabelle's mom is waiting in the car."

Oliver took off and Tobias followed him, but I hung back because something nagged at me.

Staring at Phil's project, knowing it was Phil's, well, something didn't seem right. I had this weird feeling, like maybe he wasn't being completely honest.

Not about the markers—which seemed suspicious enough—but about his whole entire project.

According to Emma, he'd only just started working on it a few days ago. Yet everything in front of me was so, well, perfect. It didn't seem possible that anyone could accomplish so much in so short a time. Not even someone as brainy and driven as Phil.

I wanted to ask him more questions but also knew that I couldn't, really—not when I wasn't supposed to know about Phil's original hamster-maze project in the first place. He'd sworn Emma to secrecy. And she'd only told me and my friends about it after swearing us to secrecy.

This was classified information squared.

But I couldn't just walk away quietly, like I didn't have a gazillion questions on the tip of my tongue. So finally I said, "When did you start working on this?"

Phil moved his hawk an inch to the left. "Six weeks ago—just like everyone else."

"Really?"

He glared at me, seemingly annoyed that I was hanging around his project. But I didn't move. I couldn't.

"Shouldn't you be heading back to your own table?" he asked finally.

"Yeah, but . . . um . . . ." Finally I just blurted it out. "What about Einstein?"

"He's dead," Phil said flatly.

"I know." I took a deep breath. I was talking about Phil's maze project but didn't want to say so. Not when he seemed so upset. "I'm really sorry."

Phil shrugged and stared at his bird carvings. "I had to buy a special metal lockbox when I buried him in my backyard, because if I put him in a regular old shoebox, the coyotes might've dug him up, and I couldn't let that happen. Not after everything he'd been through."

"That stinks," I said. "Not about the box. I mean about him dying."

"Yeah. I know."

I hesitated for a moment, hoping that Phil would

come clean, or offer up some sort of explanation, because I wanted to believe him—I truly did. But none came. So finally I just turned around and walked away.

By the time I got back to my table, I found Rachel pacing back and forth in front of it. "Where have you been?" she asked.

"Actually I was just over at Phil's and—"

Rachel cut me off. "You'll never guess what happened!"

"His project, right?" I asked, relieved that I wasn't the only one who thought something seemed fishy.

"What are you talking about?" asked Rachel.

"Nothing," I said. "What are you talking about?"

"Oh, just the fact that Caleb dumped me."

"He did?" I asked. "I'm so sorry, Rach. But wait—how is that possible when you weren't even going out?"

"I mean he dumped me as his date for the dance."

"But the dance is tomorrow night!" I cried. "Can he even do that?"

Rachel nodded. "He can and he did. It's because he thinks he's my second choice and that I only agreed to go to the dance with him because the boy I really liked had a girlfriend."

I didn't remind Rachel that this was, in fact, the case. I didn't have to because Tobias did it for me.

"You mean Erik?" he asked.

Rachel spun around and gasped. "Didn't anyone ever tell you that it's not polite to eavesdrop?"

"Um, yeah. That's why I'm not eavesdropping," Tobias replied. "You just happen to be standing right in

**162**

front of our project. I'm exactly where I'm supposed to be, and you're totally loud."

Rachel paused, seemingly taken aback. But as usual, she recovered quickly. "Well, how do you know about Erik? What did Annabelle tell you?"

"Nothing!" I promised. "We have never discussed your crush on—whoops!" I covered my mouth with my hands. "Never mind."

"Oh, please," said Tobias. "Annabelle never said a word. The entire sixth grade knows that Caleb is your second choice because it's all you've been talking about."

"That's not true!" said Rachel.

Tobias raised his eyebrows. "Then how come I overheard you complaining about him during math class last week?"

"You complained about him at the Bowl-A-Rama, too," said Oliver. "You told Claire that even though you were having fun, you wished Caleb could be more like Erik."

"You guys weren't supposed to hear that!" said Rachel. "I even whispered."

"You're kind of a loud whisperer," said Oliver.

"I am?" asked Rachel.

"Yeah," said Oliver. "And it was mean."

"He wasn't supposed to take it personally. He wasn't even supposed to hear!"

"Well, he did on both counts. And how could he not take it personally? Guys have feelings, too," said Oliver.

"Yeah!" said Tobias. "What do you think we are, dogs?"

Rachel's eyes widened with panic. She looked at me and I just shrugged.

Then she grabbed my arm and pulled me away from my lab partners. "This is terrible," she whispered fiercely (and loudly). "I can't go to the dance alone."

"You won't be alone," I said. "We're all going."

"I mean, I can't go dateless," Rachel said.

"Why not? I am and so is Yumi. You're the one who said that it doesn't really matter—that the dance will be super-fun no matter what."

"Well, of course I said that," said Rachel. "But only because I didn't want you guys feeling bad. Anyway, it's one thing to choose to go solo and quite another to be ditched by a guy."

"We'll still have fun." I couldn't believe I was trying to get Rachel excited for a dance I dreaded going to. "Maybe you could still ask Erik, since he's single."

"Erik isn't going to the dance. That's why Hannah broke up with him."

"How do you always know what's going on?" I wondered.

Rachel shrugged. "I don't always know. But in this case, my brother told me. He's friends with Caleb's brother, and they're all going snowboarding up at Mammoth this weekend. That's why Hannah got so mad. All this time she figured Erik was waiting for the right moment to ask her to the dance, when actually he never intended on going in the first place. And he didn't even bother telling her."

"That's crazy," I said.

"You guys are way too obsessed with this dance," said Tobias, wandering over to where we stood. "I told you it was stupid."

"Okay, now you're totally eavesdropping!" Rachel yelled.

"And you're totally loud!" Tobias replied.

Just then Mr. Hardis, our school principal, announced that it was time to clear out of the gym. Rachel ran back to her project to make sure it was ready for judging, and we headed out to the parking lot and woke my mom up from her nap so she could drive everyone home.

I was quiet during the whole ride, not because I was mortified by my mom falling asleep with her mouth wide open—well, not *only* for that reason—but because I couldn't take my mind off Phil.

Super-competitive Phil, who'd supposedly devoted all of his time to his hamster-maze project only to have his hamster explode, the very same Phil who had nothing to work on just three days ago.

Unless . . . could Phil have been lying to Emma? Like, maybe he'd been working on the birds of prey thing all along and he just told her he was doing a hamster maze in order to throw her off. But if that was the case, how come he begged Emma to let him go in on her and Rachel's experiment?

All this uncertainty left me with an icky feeling in the pit of my stomach.

So as soon as I got home I ran up to my room and Googled "birds of prey." Nothing familiar came up right away, but I continued my search.

Ten minutes later I found the website that Oliver, Tobias, and I had stumbled across when we first started working on our science fair project—the one that actually sold science fair projects. And listed on the third page was a project called *Night Vision in Birds of Prey*.

Gulping, I clicked on the link. And a second later it appeared. The birds carved out of soapstone, the charts and graphs, and the "see what an eagle sees" glasses. Even the calligraphy sign was for sale. The entire project cost $85 plus shipping.

It was right there on the screen in front of me: proof that Phil cheated.

## chapter twenty
### something's fishy in bird land

**P**art of me wanted to turn off my computer and act as if I'd never found this site. But I couldn't do that. I knew it would be wrong. Problem was, I didn't know what was right.

After a few moments I picked up my phone and dialed Emma's number, but before it even rang I hung up.

Phil was her boyfriend—I didn't want her to think I had it out for him. And I couldn't help but remember what Rachel told me few weeks ago, about how no one likes a snitch.

Or did that just apply to brothers and sisters?

I didn't know. Nor did I want to take that kind of risk.

Yet it wouldn't be fair to let Phil get away with buying his way to victory. I got up from my computer and flopped facedown on my bed. Pepper jumped up, too, and began licking my ear. But for once this didn't make me laugh.

When my mom called me down to dinner a while later, I still hadn't figured anything out.

"Where's Ted?" I asked.

"He has a late meeting, so it's just the two of us," she said. "I ordered a vegetarian pizza."

"What happened to cooking more often?" I asked.

"I made a salad," Mom said, serving me some.

"Looks great." I grabbed my plate, added a slice of pizza, and sat down at the kitchen table.

My mom sat down across from me. "I'm impressed with your project, Annabelle. And I'm glad I finally got to meet Oliver and Tobias. They seem like nice boys."

"Mom!" I said, embarrassed.

"What?" she asked.

I couldn't really explain to her that calling my friends "nice boys" sounded totally nerdy, so I just shook my head and said, "Nothing. Never mind."

"When does the judging take place?" she asked.

"Tomorrow morning. We're supposed to report to the gym right after first period."

"Exciting!"

I shrugged. "It's not like we have a chance of winning."

"It sounds like there were some impressive projects, but you never know."

I took a small bite of pizza even though I didn't have much of an appetite.

"You seem extra quiet tonight. Is everything okay?" she asked.

"Hey, what would you do if you caught someone cheating?"

My mom teaches high school English, so I thought she might have some sort of idea.

"Cheating at what?" she asked.

"Um. Well, say one of your students turned in a paper that was really good. Like, too good. I mean, sure this kid was smart or whatever, but you still felt suspicious. Like maybe they copied it or something. Or maybe, hypothetically, they bought it off the Internet. And you had proof, but you felt weird about turning them in because they were your friend. Or your friend's boyfriend. Or something like that."

Mom raised her eyebrows at me. "Hypothetically?"

I nodded. "Yeah. It means not real."

She laughed. "Thank you, but I know what it means. I guess I'm just surprised by the question. And it's funny you should bring up plagiarism because I had a case of it in my classroom earlier this year."

"Really?" I asked. "What happened to the guy?"

"It was a girl and she got an automatic fail. That means she has to retake the class next year with kids who are younger than her."

"Yikes! That's bad."

"Well, that's high school," said my mom. "And it wasn't her first time cheating. I would think that in middle school, for instance, a principal might be more lenient, especially for a first-time offense. Hypothetically, I mean."

I took a sip of water and finished my pizza in silence. But as I cleared my plate, my mom put her arm around me and said, "I'm so proud of you, Annabelle, for a lot of reasons. But mostly because I know that you have excellent judgment and you'll always do the right thing."

"What are you talking about?" I asked.

"Nothing in particular," said my mom. "Just, in general. I know you'll figure out what to do."

Because I didn't know how to respond to her, I faked a yawn and said good night and headed back upstairs.

But I couldn't sleep.

Phil cheated and the whole thing made me sick. I didn't want to be a snitch and I didn't want to ruin his whole life. But Tobias, Oliver, and I had worked really hard. And we followed the rules. And what about Emma and Rachel? Not to mention everyone else in the sixth grade . . .

The computer screen glowed from one corner of my room, like it was telling me I had to do something. I went back to it and studied the page. I had no doubt in my mind that Phil had bought the experiment—but every doubt regarding what I was supposed to do with that information.

So I pressed Print, not to purchase the project, but just so I could get the description—proof that it existed, that Phil didn't do the work himself.

I took the pages off the printer and slipped them into my notebook, and then tried to get some sleep.

I figured things would make more sense tomorrow. But actually, life got a gazillion times crazier.

## chapter twenty-one
### yours truly

"Happy Valentine's Day," Rachel said as soon as I swung open my front door on Friday morning. "Yumi's already on the corner, so let's go."

I grabbed my bag, yelled my good-byes to Mom, Ted, and Pepper, and followed Rachel outside and down the street, almost having to run to keep up.

"Aren't we dangerously close to duckwalking?" I asked.

"Sorry." Rachel slowed down but only for a few steps. "I can't help it. There's too much going on!"

Rachel was right, and she only knew the half of it.

"Hey, remember when you told me you didn't want to be a snitch and tell your parents that Jackson eats Slurpees for breakfast?" I asked.

"Um, I guess so," said Rachel. "How come?"

"Well, do you not want to be a snitch because he's your brother, or just because you don't want to be a snitch?"

"Both," Rachel answered. "Oh, hey, Yumi," she added, waving without even slowing down.

Yumi looked at me with raised eyebrows and I just shrugged.

"I'm so glad I never sent Caleb that gram," Rachel said. "Can you imagine how humiliating that would be? It's good we're not going to the dance together anymore. It would've been a total waste of time and not because of Erik. I'm totally over him, too. I mean, choosing to go snowboarding instead of celebrating Valentine's Day with the rest of the school? His priorities are way messed up! There's this cute guy in my social studies class—Thad. He has a girlfriend, but I don't think they're serious. She chews with her mouth open and I'm sure once he notices he'll lose interest."

Rachel kept talking but I couldn't really pay attention. Not when I had the Birds of Prey project description in my backpack. It sounded like snitching would be a bad idea, but did that mean I had to let him get away with it?

I should've called Emma last night, when I'd had the chance. I wanted to catch her before school started, but when we got to our lockers she wasn't there.

Claire was, and she gave us an update on the belts she was making. "They're super-sparkly and wide enough to wear with a dress but they'd still look cute with a tunic top or even jeans."

"Sounds great!" said Yumi.

"Not to sound stuck up," said Claire. "But they're

awesome. My sister told me I'd really outdone myself. And she wasn't even being sarcastic about it. I don't think."

Just then the bell rang and everyone scattered.

I headed to homeroom. Moments after Mr. Beller took attendance, an eighth grader walked into the room with a huge stack of cards. "The no-Candygrams have arrived," she announced.

"Oh, we don't want any," said Mr. Beller.

Some kids gasped and some shouted out their protests, to which Mr. Beller said, "I'm just kidding. Relax! I'll hand them out now." He took the stack and read the top one. "Missy?"

Everyone clapped as Missy ran to the front of the room with a big grin on her face and her hand outstretched. "For me?" she asked.

"Please save your applause for some other occasion," said Mr. Beller. "Preferably one that does not take place in my classroom. And you can all stay in your seats, as well. Now let's see. We have one for Jasper and one for Emily, two for Clara . . ."

It seemed like forever before he called my name, but once he did, I got three in a row. They were from Claire, Emma, and Rachel.

Even though I knew my friends had sent me grams, since we'd spent so much time talking about them, they still came as a nice surprise. Yes, they would've been better with candy or a balloon, but I wasn't going to complain. Not when it was so much fun reading cute messages from everyone. When my fourth one came I figured it was from Yumi—but actually I was wrong. It came from Oliver.

*To Annabelle,*
*It's been tons of fun studying bugs with you. Stay cool and have a Happy Valentine's Day!*
*Yours truly, Oliver*

I read the note three more times before it sunk in. Oliver sent me a gram. Oliver had stood in line and paid a dollar. He'd taken the time to write out a note. And apparently he thought I was cool, unless he was talking about the weather, although I don't think so because it hasn't been particularly warm out. Of course, even if he had meant the weather, it was still sweet that he cared.

My teacher called my name again and then handed me Yumi's gram.

*Hey Annabelle: Happy Valentine's Day! I hope you have your first "snow cone parking lot moment" soon! TTFN!*
*Yumi*

I laughed. Obviously her note was about kissing, which made me blush and think of Oliver. I turned back to his note, which I couldn't stop looking at until class ended.

In fact, I still had a grin on my face after class, when I headed to the gym with the rest of the sixth grade.

Time for the science fair! If I was going to do something about Phil, I had to (a) figure out what that was and (b) act fast.

But before I even made it into the gym, Rachel pulled me aside so we could compare our no-Candygrams with the rest of our friends.

"Did you get one from Oliver?" Emma asked Claire.

"Yup." Claire handed over her note, and we passed it down the line.

*To Claire, see you tomorrow.*
*Oliver*

I stared at her note, which seemed totally impersonal. Polite enough, but not so special.

"I'm so depressed," said Claire. "He didn't even mention Valentine's Day."

"It's a good note," said Rachel, although you could tell she was trying to convince everyone of this fact—including herself. "And at least you got one."

"I was hoping for 'love' or 'xoxo,' or at least one single 'o.' But to not even write 'from'?" said Claire.

"Maybe he doesn't know how to sign notes," said Emma. "Studies show that with the advent of new communication technology, the ancient art of letter writing is becoming just that—ancient."

"Huh?" asked Yumi, looking up from her phone.

175

"My point exactly," said Emma.

"But Oliver signed my gram," I said.

"Wait, what?" asked Claire.

Uh-oh. I realized too late that I'd messed up. "Nothing."

"No, you said something," said Claire. "And I think . . . Did Oliver send you a no-Candygram?"

She sounded, um, what's the opposite of happy? Reluctantly, I nodded.

"Let's see." Claire held out her hand.

I gave her the note. My friends exchanged worried glances.

Claire read it and looked up. "You got a better note."

"Well, we're good friends."

She rolled her eyes. "Okay—what's going on, Annabelle? Why do you keep saying stuff like that?"

"Like what?" I giggled out of nervousness.

She just glared at me.

"Um, can I have my note back?" I asked.

"You're always like, Oliver this and Oliver that. We had ginger cookies at Oliver's house. Oliver is such a great artist. He can play cricket, too. It's so popular in Jamaica."

Claire made her voice sound extra high and squeaky, like she was imitating my voice, except I don't sound like that at all.

And she still hadn't given me back Oliver's note.

I stood up straighter. "I don't know what you're talking about," I said. But even as the words left my mouth, I had to wonder, did I? Maybe I hadn't hidden my feelings as well as I'd thought. But no. This wasn't my fault and I didn't do anything wrong. "You're the one who asked me to talk to him. And he is a great artist. And we are partners. That's the only reason we sent each other no-Candygrams."

"Wait, what?" asked Claire. "You sent Oliver a no-Candygram, too?"

"Yes, but its no biggie because—"

"It's no biggie? It's HUGE!" Claire yelled.

I looked at Yumi, who stared at her cell phone. Rachel kicked at something on the ground and Emma checked her watch, like it was the most fascinating thing in the world. My friends looked like they wanted to be someplace else. Anyplace else. And I didn't blame them.

I'd seen Claire annoyed with her sister for staining her favorite white T-shirt, upset when she'd gotten a C+ on a test she thought she'd aced. But all that paled in comparison to this moment when Claire—red faced and eyes narrowed—glared at me with a look of pure rage. "I cannot believe you sent him a no-Candygram!"

"We're lab partners, so I just thought it would be nice."

"Really?" asked Claire. "Tobias is your partner, too. Did you send one to him?"

I opened my mouth to explain but no words came out.

Everyone stayed quiet, waiting for me to say something.

"It's different," I finally admitted.

Claire waved my note in the air. "That's my point exactly. It's different because you're not in love with him."

"I'm not in love with anyone." My voice cracked in a way that was obvious even to me—of course I was.

"Okay, look me in the eye and tell me you have no feelings for Oliver. That you're not trying to steal him."

I raised my gaze to Claire's, shivering at their eerie, angry glow. "I'm not trying to steal him," I said carefully. "How could I do that when you guys aren't even together?"

Someone gasped. I don't know who, but it didn't matter.

Claire blinked at me, stunned and hurt. "I can't believe you said that." She spoke in a whisper, like a wounded puppy, and for some reason this annoyed me.

"Well, it's true," I said.

"Exactly—no thanks to you!" Claire crumpled my note, threw it at my feet, and stormed off.

## chapter twenty-two
### explosions of a different kind

The judging was about to start, so there wasn't time to chase after Claire. And even if there had been, I didn't know what I'd say to her. She wasn't wrong about everything. I did like Oliver. But she definitely misunderstood what was going on. I never tried to steal him and I *had* wanted to help her. I truly did. It's just, well, I also wanted Oliver for myself.

It was all too complicated and, anyway, I had to find Phil before it was too late.

I rushed past my project with a quick wave to Tobias and Oliver. Then I pushed my way through the crowd until I made it to Phil, who stood in front of his display. He was all dressed up in khakis and a shirt with a collar. Excited and probably assuming that he'd not only get away with plagiarizing, but also that he'd win first prize. It made me feel bad for what I was about to do but, at the same time, annoyed that I had to.

"Hi!" I said.

Phil's eyes seemed to darken when he saw me. "Isn't your project at the other end of the gym?"

"Yeah, but we need to talk." I took a deep breath. "I found something I need to show you."

And since I didn't know what to say next, I just pulled the pages I'd printed out of my bag and handed them over.

"What's this?" asked Phil, his face turning bright red—like he didn't need me to answer.

"Um, I think you know."

Phil looked up. "I've never seen this before. What a crazy coincidence. There's no way I—"

"Stop!" I raised one hand like a traffic cop. "We both know that's not true."

He opened his mouth to protest further but then gave up. "Geez, Annabelle. I didn't realize you had it out for me."

"I don't," I said. "This isn't personal. It's just not right. You can't cheat. It's not fair to everyone else. And by the way—I didn't turn you in."

"Good, because Ms. Roberts already said she was impressed. And I've worked harder than anyone here. If only Einstein hadn't died. Or if he'd died sooner and I'd had more time." He blinked and wiped his eyes. "Never mind. That's a rotten thing to say."

"It is," I told him. "And this is a rotten thing to do. You've got to drop out of the fair."

"It's too late," said Phil. "And if Ms. Roberts doesn't know, no one else will figure it out, either."

"But *you* know," I said. "And you can still walk away. The science fair isn't mandatory. So just pack up your stuff and get out of here."

He looked at me sideways. "And what? If I don't, you'll tell on me?"

"I don't want to," I said. "So please don't make me."

Phil stared from me to his project.

"Come on, Phil. You know this isn't fair."

"Know what's not fair? The fact that my last project was so awesome."

I stood my ground and stared him down. And there were a few moments there when it seemed like he'd stubbornly persist. But finally he sighed and took down his fancy wooden sign. Then he folded up the charts and graphs and dumped the bird models into his backpack and walked out of the gym, his backpack slung over slumped shoulders.

Even though he'd done what I'd asked—what he had to do, really—I still felt awful.

"Where's Phil?" Emma asked, hurrying over a minute later. "I just came by to wish him luck because the judging is about to start and—" She looked around. "What happened to his project? This is Phil's table, right?"

I hadn't planned on telling anyone what happened, but Emma was one of my best friends, not to mention Phil's girlfriend, so I figured she had a right to know.

"He just withdrew his project," I said. "Because it wasn't really his."

"What?" asked Emma.

"They sell that Birds of Prey experiment online."

Emma's eyes got wide. "No way!"

"It's true. I figured it out last night and I couldn't just let Phil— Wait! Emma?"

Rather than stick around for my explanation, she'd run after Phil.

I had a clear view of Emma and Rachel's booth from mine, which is how I knew that Emma didn't come back. Not for the judging and not for the announcement of the winners, which is too bad since her group won first prize.

Rachel and Emma were heading to Space Camp. And as happy as I was for them, I felt insanely jealous that my best friends would be leaving me behind. Even though, it turns out, Space Camp only lasts one week.

But I guess things could've been worse.

At least we won second prize. Yes, that's right. Me and Tobias and Oliver each won a ten-dollar gift certificate to the International House of Pancakes.

"Who wants to go away to Space Camp when you can have a round of Swedish pancakes with lemon butter?" I joked with Rachel after school that day.

She cracked up. "Um, me."

"Right. Congratulations, then!"

"Thanks!" she replied. "Hey, where were you at lunch?"

"Library. I had to study for a test." I felt bad about lying but I couldn't tell her the truth—that I'd been hiding from my friends because I figured they were all mad. And that even now I was surprised she was willing to talk to me.

But here she was, looking at her watch and making plans for tomorrow night. "The dance starts at 6:00, which means we should leave at 5:54, so we can get there at 6:04—casually late but not obviously so. Everyone's coming to my place at 5:00 so we can get ready. Sound good?"

"We're still doing that?"

"Of course," said Rachel. "And you know what? I'm glad I don't have a date. We'll have way more fun this way. Boys make things too complicated. Who needs all that drama?"

"Speaking of drama—how's Claire?"

"Oh, she's pretty mad," said Rachel.

"Really?" I asked.

"No," said Rachel. "Furious is more like it."

"Do you think I should apologize?"

"What do you think?" Rachel replied.

It was a good question, but not one I could answer yet.

## chapter twenty-three
### sparkly belts, the big dance,
### and freeze tag

I found the perfect outfit for the big dance—tight black jeans and a blue checked button-down shirt. My mom blow-dried my hair smooth and shiny. And she even let me borrow her favorite silver necklace. But looking good on the outside hardly mattered. Not with half my friends mad at me.

When I walked across the street to Rachel's on Saturday night, Emma was just getting out of her mom's car.

"Hey!" I said, running to catch up to her. "I've been calling you since yesterday."

"Yeah, I know, but I was too upset to talk."

"Sorry about Phil," I said. "I know he's your boy-friend, but I couldn't let him get away with cheating. And having one friend mad at me is bad enough so I hope you'll—"

"Wait, you think I'm mad at you?" Emma asked.

"It seemed that way at the science fair. You took off before they even announced the winners."

"Because I didn't want to cry in front of the entire

sixth grade, but that's not your fault. Phil is the problem. I still can't believe he cheated."

"I know. It's bad. But he's probably not thinking straight, since Einstein's death."

"That's what he tried to tell me, but it's no excuse."

"So you guys are fighting?" I asked.

"Not anymore," said Emma. "I dumped him. No way could I go out with a cheater."

"I'm sorry, Emma."

"Me, too." She sighed. "But it's not just about the science fair. Things have been weird with Phil for a while. I used to think he was a super-nice guy with a tiny competitive streak. But the way he's been acting . . . It's more like he's a super-competitive guy with a tiny streak of niceness. And that's not good enough."

"Well, at least you get to go to Space Camp."

"I know. It's going to be awesome. And I owe you one. If it weren't for you, Phil would've won, probably. And then I'd be stuck eating Swedish pancakes. No offense."

"No offense?" I asked. "Um, sorry, but that's totally offensive."

Emma gasped and covered her mouth with her hands. "Whoops—sorry. I forgot I told you about that theory."

I laughed. "Don't worry about it. I'm totally jealous—but you guys deserve to go."

She gave me a quick hug, and then we climbed the steps to Rachel's house.

Our other friends were already upstairs. And even though the new Lady Gaga single blared from Rachel's computer, the room felt eerily silent as soon as I stepped into it.

"You guys look great." I smiled big and tried not to act as awkward as I felt.

Rachel and Yumi both said thanks, but Claire turned away, like I wasn't even there.

Everyone continued getting ready. Rachel changed out of a jean skirt and into a cotton one, stepping around the rejected outfits that covered her floor.

Yumi applied lip gloss in the mirror.

"Cute color," said Emma, sitting down next to her. "What's it called?"

"Depressed Heiress," Yumi replied, puckering her lips.

Finally I realized I must look weird just standing there like a wax version of myself, so I sat down next to Claire and checked out her belt. It was turquoise and sparkly—a nice contrast to her black dress. Yumi wore a red one with dark wash jeans and a white V-neck shirt. Rachel's was silver, which would've gone with any of the six outfits she was considering.

"These belts are amazing." Even though I spoke with sincerity, my words sounded forced—even to me. "I can't believe you made them."

Rather than answer me, Claire stared into the mirror and pretended like she needed to concentrate on putting in her earrings. But I knew she was faking.

Claire pierced her ears when she was nine. She didn't need the mirror—she just didn't want to acknowledge me.

I pressed my lips together, wishing we could talk alone because I didn't want to do this in front of an audience. But I needed to get my apology over with.

"I'm sorry I never told you about my crush on Oliver," I said. "I know I messed up."

"Know what?" asked Rachel. "I need to show you guys something in the garage. Just Emma and Yumi, though." She grabbed their hands and turned to me and Claire. "You two stay here."

My friends giggled as they hurried out of the room, slamming the door behind them.

Claire rolled her eyes and then turned down the music.

"I'm really sorry," I said again.

"Whatever. It's not like I couldn't tell you had a massive crush on Oliver."

"Really?" I asked.

"It was obvious from the moment I told everyone. As soon as I mentioned his name you got this panicked look on your face."

"I guess I should've said something."

"You guess?" Claire laughed, not kindly. "There's no guessing. You totally should have—especially since I asked you, flat out, if you liked him."

"Yeah, you're right. But I didn't *choose* to like the same guy as you. It just happened—accidentally. And

I know it seemed sneaky, sending him that no-Candygram without telling you guys. I didn't mean to do it behind your back. I just felt weird talking about it because I thought you'd be mad if you knew I liked him."

"I am mad," said Claire. "But only because you weren't honest with me. And also because I can tell Oliver doesn't like me. Not as anything more than a friend, I mean."

"I'm sorry," I said. And then I took a deep breath and decided to be even more honest. "I mean, I'm sorry the boy you like doesn't like you back. But given that he's also the boy I like, well, it makes everything more complicated."

"No kidding," said Claire.

Just then the door opened. Rachel, Emma, and Yumi all peeked in.

"Are we finally okay now?" asked Rachel.

Claire let out a laugh. "You say that like you haven't been listening at the door."

"Who me?" asked Rachel, walking back into the room.

We all cracked up.

"Yeah, we're good," Claire said. "Except for one thing." She pulled two more sparkly belts from her bag and handed them to me and Emma. Mine was blue and hers was yellow, and once Rachel decided on an outfit (her shiny black pants and a red top) we were ready to go and looking fabulous.

Before I knew it we were there—at the big Valentine's Day dance.

My stomach felt all jumpy as we filed out of Rachel's mom's minivan and into the gym.

Pink and red streamers hung from the ceiling. Hip-hop music blasted from the DJ's speakers. A strobe light flashed, so everyone seemed to move in slow motion. Some kids danced and others wandered around, as if looking for something they couldn't quite find.

"This is awesome!" said Yumi.

"I can't believe we're finally here," Emma said.

Claire glanced around the room nervously. Looking for Oliver, I realized, with a tinge of sadness.

Soon Taylor's date, Jimmy Brontini, walked over and asked her to dance. Then Jesse asked his friend to dance, and soon other kids started asking their dates to dance. And suddenly, the middle of the room was filled with enough dancing couples that the dance actually looked like a dance as opposed to a big train terminal with lots of lost-looking kids wandering around.

Meanwhile, my friends and I stood off to the side—not one of us dancing or even swaying.

"We can't be wallflowers all night," Rachel said finally. "Someone do something." She turned to Claire. "Where's Oliver?"

"Over there." Claire pointed to the corner of the room, where Oliver, Tobias, Sanjay, and Jonathan were playing freeze tag.

"Aren't you gonna ask him to dance?" asked Rachel.

"Shouldn't he ask me?" Claire wondered.

"He's probably too shy," said Yumi.

"I say ask him. Since he is your date."

Claire looked at me, surprised that those words came from my mouth, and I didn't blame her. I surprised myself.

"Go ahead," I said.

She ran her fingers through her bangs, took a deep breath, and walked across the room. It was too loud to hear what they were saying, but things must've gone well because moments later they walked to the middle of the dance floor and danced.

And watching them wasn't so bad.

Well, it wasn't torture.

Meaning I've definitely experienced worse things.

Like getting a cavity filled, or being swept underwater by a massive wave, or falling off my bike and twisting my ankle, or scraping my knee—or this one time when I tumbled off my ten-speed and twisted my ankle *and* scraped my knee.

My point is, those things are all worse than—

On second thought, never mind.

It turns out that actually I'd rather be doing any of those things if it meant I wouldn't have to watch one of my best friends dance with my crush.

The song seemed to last forever, too, but it did end, eventually. And I survived.

Then a fast song came on and Rachel said, "I'm sick of standing around. Let's dance."

So we all started swaying and then full-on dancing—swinging our arms and stomping our feet and spinning around, and by the time the next song came on we were having a blast.

Ten minutes later, the DJ played a slow song, so we moved off the dance floor. "Hey, want me to take your picture so you can text it to Nathan?" I asked Yumi. "You look so great."

"That's okay," she said.

"Hey, how come you're not on your phone now?" asked Emma. "Are you guys fighting?"

"Nope," said Yumi. "But his parents got their long-distance bill and flipped out. They took away his phone and he's grounded, so now we're only allowed to IM on weekends and only for ten minutes at a time."

"That stinks!" I said.

Yumi shrugged. "It seemed bad at first, but it's okay. Turns out it's more fun hanging out with friends who actually live in the same time zone."

When the next fast song came on, we headed back to the dance floor.

And before I knew it, I forgot to check on Claire and Oliver every two minutes.

In fact, she totally surprised me when she showed up later that night with her blue eyes sparkling and her cheeks flushed.

"Where's your date?" Emma asked.

Claire shrugged. "A bunch of guys are playing touch football outside. I think he's with them."

"But he's your date," said Rachel. "That's so immature! Do you want me to go get him?"

Claire shook her head. "No, I'd rather hang out with you guys, anyway."

Rachel and Yumi did a tango while Emma clapped. Claire grinned and grabbed my hands and we both started spinning until we were dizzy, and once we stopped we stumbled and laughed and then started dancing again.

Which is when I realized something. All this time I'd been so worried about not having a date. But I totally missed the most obvious thing.

I wasn't dateless at all.

I had the four best dates in the entire school.

## chapter twenty-four
### are pancake allergies real? and other questions i'm not yet qualified to answer.

I got to science so early on Monday Ms. Roberts wasn't even there yet. Plenty of students were, though. A bunch of them goofed around in the back of the room, but Oliver was already at our table.

I sat down next to him and said hi.

Rather than answer me, he slid over a cookie.

"Your mom made them?" I asked.

"Nope. I did."

I took a bite. "These are the best!"

He nodded. "Yeah, I know."

"And it's good that you're not modest about it," I joked.

"It's important to be straightforward about cookies," he replied. "And speaking of that—or of food, at least—have you used your gift certificate yet? For the pancake house, I mean."

"I knew what you meant. And no. Not yet. You?"

He shook his head, then clicked his pen open and shut a few times, fast. Staring at it hard, like he was trying to see through the plastic to the inner spring mechanism. "Want to go next weekend?"

"Really?" I asked, thinking—wait. Did Oliver just ask me out on a date?

"Yeah. We can celebrate our victory."

Oh, right. Of course he didn't just suggest a date— just a science fair team reunion. Rats!

"Cool," I said. "You mean all three of us, right?" I glanced toward the back of the room, where Tobias had Jonathan in a headlock. He yelled at him to scream uncle, but Jonathan, red-faced and sputtering, refused.

Oliver looked too and cringed. "Um, maybe just the two of us could go?"

"Okay, sure!" I said, perhaps too quickly.

"Yeah, Tobias is allergic to pancakes." Oliver turned back around and clicked his pen a few more times.

"Really?" I asked.

"Yup. But, uh, don't tell him I told you because he's embarrassed about it."

Just then Ms. Roberts walked into the room and everyone hurried to their seats. After congratulating me and Oliver and Tobias on our science fair victory, she began her lecture.

I opened up my notebook and tried to take notes. Honestly, I did. But no way could I concentrate. Not with so many questions racing through my mind.

Was Tobias really allergic to pancakes? Or was Oliver just kidding? Pancake allergies aren't even that funny, when you think about it. And Oliver has a pretty good sense of humor. So was it true? Or did he make it up because he didn't want Tobias tagging along?

And if so, was that because he's sick of hanging out with Tobias or because our pancake outing is supposed to be our big first date? Not that it had to be big. And not that pancakes are so romantic. Maybe we were just going as friends. Or maybe Oliver really did like me. I mean, obviously he liked me, but did he *like* me like me or just like me?

I sneaked a sideways glance at him. And a second later, he caught me staring.

I turned away fast, but not before I noticed his small grin. The kind that told me this: The answers to all my questions? They may not come for a while, but once they did, they were going to be good.

## acknowledgments

Yay Bloomsbury! Thanks very much to Michelle Nagler, Caroline Abbey, Melanie Cecka, Jennifer Healey, Melissa Kavonic, Nicole Gastonguay, Donna Mark, Vanessa Nuttry, Rebecca Mancini, Deb Shapiro, Beth Eller, and Diana Blough.

Thank you, Laura Langlie, Bill Contardi, and Coe Booth.

And mega-thanks to Jim, Leo, and Lucy, who showed up just in time.

Don't miss Leslie Margolis's newest
Maggie Brooklyn mystery!

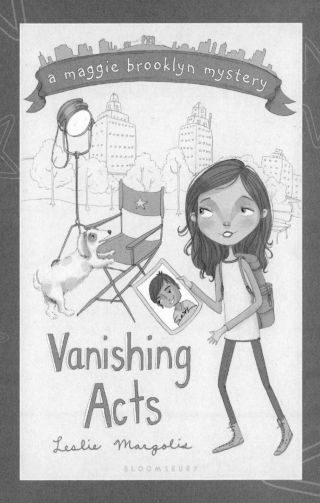

a maggie brooklyn mystery

Vanishing
Acts

Leslie Margolis

BLOOMSBURY

Action! A cute young heartthrob and a new movie
filming in Maggie's neighborhood bring drama both
on and off set. Read on for a sneak peek.

If I were the type to travel in a pack, like a wolf or one of those girls with a bunch of best friends, Sonya and Beatrix would be in it, no question. They're in the seventh grade, too, and just as sweet and funny as Lucy. But since I am a one-best-friend type of girl, they're the next best thing.

And that's okay, because I don't think they'd want to be best, best friends with me, either, since I'm not obsessed with Seth Ryan.

Like most kids I know, he's my favorite movie star, for the obvious reasons: cute, a great actor, and he donated the proceeds of his last movie to the ASPCA. In other words, he's a puppy lover with puppy-dog eyes.

I've seen most of his movies. The last two I even went to on opening night.

But it's not like I'd start a Seth Ryan fan club.

Or launch a website devoted to his life and work.

Or design T-shirts with his face on them.

Or have meetings after school twice a week to plan even more Seth Ryan superfan–related activities.

Yet that's exactly what Beatrix and Sonya have been doing.

Beatrix has been into Seth Ryan for over a year. For Sonya, he's a new obsession. She'd only just recently replaced the unicorn posters on her bedroom walls with pinups of him.

"Who's Seth Ryan?" I asked with a straight face.

"Not funny, Maggie," said Beatrix. "You can't joke about the most famous movie star in the world. He's off-limits!"

"How are you guys going to be in his movie?" asked Lucy.

"Not just Sonya and me," said Beatrix. "All of us. They're filming in the neighborhood and they need extras, immediately."

"That sounds amazing," Lucy said.

"Almost too amazing," I added.

"That's exactly what I thought," said Sonya. "But I know it's true, because it's all over the Internet."

"Isn't that where you read they were tearing down our school to put in a giant cupcake factory?" I asked.

"It wasn't a giant cupcake factory," Sonya replied. "It was a regular-size factory that specialized in baking giant cupcakes."

"Obviously," said Lucy, smiling at me.

"You guys, this is totally legit," said Sonya as she unpacked her lunch. "I promise. I walked by Second Street on my way to school, and it's already closed to regular traffic. This giant truck rolled up and unloaded six humongous trailers. You know—the kind movie stars use as dressing rooms. And then another truck came, and it was filled with giant lights and movie cameras."

This wasn't hugely shocking. People film stuff in our neighborhood all the time. Especially on Second Street. In the past six months, they'd roped off the street for a Tom Cruise movie and a Trident gum commercial. But as for the rest of it? It seemed too good to be true.

"If they really needed extras, don't you think they would've figured it out before today?" I asked.

"They had," said Beatrix. "Or at least they thought they had. They were going to use a crowd in a box."

"What's that?" asked Lucy.

"It's an inflatable crowd," Beatrix explained. "It's when they use blow-up people to save money so they don't have to deal with real extras."

"Inflatable extras are much less complicated," said Sonya. "Except on days with high winds."

"They all blew away," Beatrix said. "And there's no time to get new plastic."

Suddenly everything clicked into place. "So that

explains that puffy dude that plowed into me this morning."

"Huh?" asked my friends.

I told them about my run-in with the blow-up doll. "We saw a few, but I had no idea they were part of a whole gang."

"There were thirty, apparently," said Beatrix. "Kind of an expensive mistake."

"So where's the doll?" asked Lucy.

"We stuffed him in a trash can on Garfield," I explained. "Finn wanted to keep him, but I said no way."

"Finn is so funny," said Lucy.

My brother is a lot of things: quiet, smart, and good at soccer and video games and making omelets. Sweet when he wants to be, and, at times, slightly clueless. But funny? I don't think so.

"Think the dummy's still there?" asked Sonya. "He'd be a cool addition to our collection of Seth Ryan memorabilia."

"I don't think a blow-up doll would fit in the scrapbook," said Beatrix.

"I mean if we deflated him," Sonya said. "Obviously."

"He was huge," I said. "Taller than me and probably as wide as Finn and me put together, so even flat and folded it would be a stretch."

"We need to get a third scrapbook anyway," Sonya said.

"Unless we just move all of the existing stuff to a bigger binder," said Beatrix. She turned to Lucy and me. "We can't seem to agree."

Lucy and I grinned at each other, not at all surprised. It seemed like Beatrix and Sonya disagreed about everything relating to Seth Ryan: which movie was his best, how often they should e-mail him, where to hold their next fan club meeting, whether or not they should continue calling themselves a fan club, considering the fact that they were the only two members . . .

"And it's not like we can vote on it," said Sonya. "We need a third person to break the tie, but there's no way we're going to try asking anyone at school again."

Last month, Beatrix and Sonya tried recruiting new kids to their club. Lucy and I were obvious choices, but we're both too busy. So they put up a bunch of signs around campus. It seemed like a no-brainer, since every girl here, practically, is in love with Seth Ryan. Boys like him, too. They'd never say so out loud, but their hairstyles prove it.

Of course, it didn't work out so well. Within an hour, their signs got covered with mean graffiti. People drew funny mustaches and devil's horns on his close-ups. They blacked out his eyes and half his teeth and scrawled obnoxious messages like *Seth Ryan Super Nerds* and *Dorks R Us!* and *This is Dum*, which is particularly insulting, because obviously there is nothing dumber than being called dumb by someone who can't even spell the word "dumb."

The takeaway being, it's cool to like Seth Ryan—almost everyone at school does—but it's not cool to be in an official fan club. All admiring must be done in an unofficial capacity. Beatrix and Sonya learned that the hard way.

"I'll bet they need guys, too," said Lucy. "Maybe Finn wants to sign up."

"They didn't specify, but I'm sure they do. You should definitely ask him," said Beatrix.

I shook my head. "There's no way. If I even mention the possibility, he'll laugh in my face. Last month after I rented *Vampire's Retreat* he made fun of me for a week."

"Maybe I'll ask him," said Lucy. "I don't think he'd laugh at me."

And before I could stop her, she'd jumped up from the table and was gone, her single braid bouncing on her back as she hurried across the cafeteria.

I turned to my friends. "Have you guys noticed Lucy acting weird lately?"

"Yes," said Sonya. "But no weirder than usual. So are you in?"

"It sounds fun, but I have to work after school."

"This is work," said Beatrix. "I heard they're paying eighty bucks a day just to stand around and be on camera. Filming starts tomorrow. The movie is called *Vanished*. Since we're under eighteen, we've got to get our parents' permission, but I already printed out extra release forms." She slammed a piece of paper down in front of me. "Here. Have your parents read and sign it. And report to work tomorrow at four p.m. sharp. Don't be late. Who knows how many people are going to show? Hundreds, I'm sure."

I looked down at the form. It had lots of fine print. I looked back up at my friends. "I don't think I can do it. I'm pretty busy with my dogs, and I didn't even tell you about my new mystery."

Sonya stared at me, her big brown eyes even wider than usual. "That's really cool, but can't it wait a few days? How many times do you think an opportunity like this is going to come up?"

Beatrix nodded. "Please sign up. It's going to be crazy fun!"

I told them I'd think about it, figuring Beatrix knew what she was talking about. Being an extra did seem like it would be crazy fun.

At least that's what I'd thought at the time.

Turns out we were only half right.

Jimmy Bruch

**leslie margolis** promises that no bugs were harmed in the making of this book. She is the author of two previous Annabelle Unleashed novels, *Boys Are Dogs* and *Girls Acting Catty*, as well as two Maggie Brooklyn Mysteries, *Girl's Best Friend* and *Vanishing Acts*. She lives with her family in Brooklyn, New York. Definitely visit her online for games, quizzes, and more!

www.lesliemargolis.com

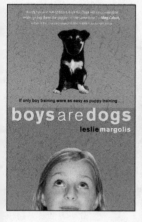

Disappearing dogs? Missing boys?
Not when Maggie Brooklyn Sinclair
is on the case . . .

"There's appeal galore here. . . . The kind of
good, solid mystery that slides neatly into a
weekend or summer evening." —BCCB

www.maggiebrooklyn.com